THE GUNSMITH

455

Brotherly Love

Books by J.R. Roberts
(Robert J. Randisi)

The Gunsmith series

Lady Gunsmith series

Angel Eyes series

Tracker series

Mountain Jack Pike series

COMING SOON!

The Gunsmith
456 – The Daughter of Jean Lafitte

For more information visit:
www.SpeakingVolumes.us

THE GUNSMITH

455

Brotherly Love

J.R. Roberts

SPEAKING VOLUMES, LLC
NAPLES, FLORIDA
2020

Brotherly Love

ISBN 978-1-64540-180-3

Chapter One

If Clint Adams had a home, it was Labyrinth, Texas. Well, it was the closest thing he had to a home.

He had a regular room in the Labyrinth Hotel, he had a friend—Rick Hartman—he knew Eclipse would be well taken care of in the local livery, and while he didn't have a regular woman there, he did have women, regularly.

The women, more often than not, came from Rick Hartman's Saloon, but they were never ordered or instructed to sleep with Clint. Usually, he connected with one of them, and it happened. That was probably because he spent most of his spare time in that saloon.

People in town knew him, and that he was friends with Rick, but the only folks he interacted with either worked in the livery, or a local restaurant. And every so often, the woman he connected with was a waitress, rather than a saloon girl. And his visits to town were usually far enough apart that, when he returned, the saloon girls and waitresses in town were new.

But this trip, it was a little different. After he took care of Eclipse, and dropped his gear in his hotel room, he went to the barbershop for a haircut and a bath. That was where he met Melanie Jones, the lady barber . . .

***

When he walked into the barber shop and saw the woman, he stopped short.

"Whatsamatta," she asked, "never had your hair cut by a woman before?"

"Huh? Uh, no, as a matter of fact, I haven't."

"Well," she said, "there's a first time for everythin', right?"

She gestured toward the chair.

"I was going to have a bath first, in the back," he said. "There are still bathtubs in the back, right?"

"Right," she said, "but it's better to have the haircut first, then the bath washes away those nasty little hairs that get all over you."

She gestured to her chair, again.

"Come on," she said. "People see you in my chair, I might actually start to get some customers. Whatayasay?"

"Okay," he said, approaching the chair.

"I'm Melanie," she said.

"Clint."

They shook hands and he sat in the chair. Up close he saw some lines in her face that put her in her late thirties. She had long dark hair pulled back in a ponytail, a full body, and she smelled of something fresh and clean.

"So, are you new?" he asked, as she covered him.

"Yup," she said. "I took over the place last month."

"And no customers, yet?"

"One or two," she said, "but not enough."

"How are you living, then?" he asked. "And eating?"

"I had some money saved," she said, as she removed his hat. "I'm still livin' off that. You keepin' that gunbelt on?"

"I am."

"Okay." She started cutting his hair, then stopped and looked at him in the mirror. "Wait, you said Clint? Are you Clint Adams?"

"I am."

"I heard that you come to town from time to time," she said, going back to cutting. "Stayin' long, this time?"

"I never know," Clint said. "I go where the wind blows me."

"That must be a wonderful way to live."

"Sometimes it is," he said, "and sometimes it isn't."

"Must be hard to make friends," she said, "have relationships."

"I can make friends," he said, "but you're right about the other thing."

When she moved around in front of him and settled between his legs, he found himself looking down the front of her shirt at her bulging cleavage. She didn't notice,

3

though, as her attention seemed to be completely on his hair.

When she moved around to the other side, she leaned against him once or twice, so that he could feel her heat, and how solid she was. She wasn't a pretty woman, but she had violet eyes, and a very interesting face. Her nose might have been too long, and her mouth too wide, but together they presented an interesting picture.

When she finished with his hair she asked, "Howzat?"

He looked in the mirror and said, "It looks fine."

"Want a shave?"

"No, I'm good."

She removed the cover from him, shook it out so that the loose hair hit the floor. As he got out of the chair, he noticed some people looking in the window, curiously.

"I'll go and get your bath ready then," she said. "Hot?"

"Very," he said.

"Gimme fifteen minutes," she said, and walked to the back.

Chapter Two

Clint eased into the hot water slowly, letting the heat sink into his bones and muscles. On a chair, right next to the tub, was his gun and gunbelt.

He could feel the miles he had put on his body melting away. So much of his time was spent on the trail that most of his baths were taken in cold lakes, streams or water holes. This was a pleasure to be enjoyed.

His eyes were closed when he heard the door to the room open. Grabbing for his gun, he sat up and then saw the barber, Melanie, entering with a steaming bucket.

"I thought you might like some more hot water," she said. "May I pour?"

"Sure," he said, "sounds good." He set the gun down on the chair, but stayed alert lest someone else come bursting into the room behind her.

That was not the case, though, as she poured the extra water into his tub. Once again, the water grew hot enough to bake the aches out of him.

"There ya go," she said, straightening. "Gimme a call if you want anythin' else."

For a brief moment Clint imagined the full-bodied woman stripping down and climbing into the tub with him, but instead she simply walked out and closed the door behind her.

He finished his bath, rising when the water once again grew tepid, dried and dressed, then strapped on his gun. When he went back out to the barbershop, Melanie had another customer in her chair, a small boy about six.

"Mr. Adams, meet Billy, my favorite customer."

"Hello, Billy," he said.

The boy stared at him with wide eyes and said, "Wow, you're the Gunsmith."

"That's right," he said.

"Billy's my only regular customer," she told Clint. "His momma sends him in here once a week."

"She don't like my hair gettin' too long," Billy said.

"She just wants you to look handsome all the time," Melanie told him.

"Aw, Melanie . . ." Billy said, blushing.

"Well," Clint said to them both, "if you're good enough for Billy, you're good enough for me. I'll be your second regular customer."

He paid her for his haircut, and bath.

"I appreciate the business, Clint," she said, pocketing the money.

Clint left the barbershop and headed for Rick's Saloon.

***

Rick had new girls working the floor, and a new bartender.

"I expected you earlier," Rick said. "I heard you rode into town."

"I needed a bath and a haircut, first," Clint said, sitting across from his friend. It was early and there were only a few customers in the place. Three saloon girls were standing at the end of the bar, talking amongst themselves.

"Ah, then you met our new barber," Rick said.

"I did."

"What'd you think?"

"She did a good job," he said, "and kept my bath water hot."

"No," Rick said, with a smile, "I mean, what did you think?" He raised his eyebrows.

"She's very attractive," Clint said.

"Earthy, don't you think?" Rick asked.

"That word hadn't come to mind for me, but yeah, I suppose so."

"It's nice to have a real woman in town," Rick said.

"What's wrong with your new girls?" Clint asked.

"That's just it, they're girls," Rick said.

7

"Does that mean that none of those three are warming your bed, these days?"

"Don't be ridiculous," Rick said. "It's the brunette, Patty."

"Ah."

"She's the oldest," Rick said. "Twenty-eight."

"A little old for you, isn't she?" Clint asked. His friend was getting close to fifty, and usually liked younger women.

"I don't know," Rick said. "The young ones seem to be annoying me, these days."

"How?" Clint asked.

"When they talk," Rick said. "They're fine until they talk, then you realize how stupid they are."

"So older and smarter women, these days?" Clint asked.

"I suppose that's what I've worked my way up to," Rick said. "What about you?"

"I try to stay away from young ones."

"Because they're stupid?"

"Because they make me feel like a dirty old man," Clint complained.

Rick had waved at the bartender when Clint entered, and the man came over now with a pot of coffee and two cups.

"This is Shiloh, Clint," Rick said.

The man seemed to be in his thirties, had a quick, infectious smile.

"Pleased to meet you, Mr. Adams," he said, and went back to the bar.

"I'm not used to you having handsome young bartenders around, Rick," Clint said. "Which girl is his?"

"The blonde," Rick said. "She's the youngest, at twenty-two."

"And the redhead?"

"Twenty-five," Rick said, "and dumb as a stump."

"Huh," Clint said, pouring out two cups of coffee.

Rick picked his up and sat back.

"How long are you gonna be here for this time?" he asked Clint.

"I don't know," Clint said. "I've been on the trail a long time. I might need a good rest."

"Well," Rick said, "it won't be a chore, havin' you around for a while."

"Thanks for that," Clint said.

"Steak tonight at Harbor's?" Rick asked.

"Harbor's?"

"A new steakhouse," Rick said. "The town's growing, you know."

"Yes," Clint said, unhappily, "I noticed that as I rode in. Sure, steak sounds good."

"Good," Rick said, "now tell me what you've been up to? All I get are cryptic telegrams asking for information. Tell me what's actually been going on."

Chapter Three

Over coffee Clint regaled Rick with stories about where he had been and what he'd done since the last time he was in Labyrinth. Later that evening, he continued over steaks at Harbor's Steakhouse.

"Who or what is Harbor?" Clint asked, as they were seated in the crowded diningroom.

"Edward Harbor," Rick said. "He opened two months ago, and he's doin' pretty well."

"How's the food?" Clint asked.

"I'll let you be the judge of that," Rick said, as a waiter came with their plates.

They suspended conversation while they cut into their steaks and consumed them with mugs of beer.

When they were done and waiting for dessert, Rick asked, "Well?"

"Not bad," Clint said. "The steak's edible, but the thing here are the vegetables. I don't think I've ever had carrots cooked like this before."

"I know," Rick said. "They melt in your mouth."

When the waiter brought their pie and coffee, they stopped talking again.

After Clint had eaten his peach, and Rick his apple, Clint asked, "Are you heading back to work?"

"Of course," Rick said. "Where else would I go?"

"We've talked about me relaxing," Clint said. "When do you relax?"

"When I'm in my saloon," Rick said, "I am relaxed. I'm home." He pushed his chair back. "And if you come home with me now, I'll let you have a free beer."

Standing, Clint said, "That's an offer I can't refuse."

***

Clint had his free beer at Rick's Place, then another while Rick saw to his business. In the evenings, he had extra help on, two burly men who could assist him in keeping the peace in his home.

There was gambling going on, but Clint was content standing at the bar, watching the action. He had a third beer, and then the days on the trail, and the hot bath, caught up with him. He felt his eyes closing, and knew he had to get to his hotel before he fell asleep on his feet.

He said goodnight to Rick, and they agreed to see each other at breakfast, which Rick usually had right there in his home.

Outside he found the streets of Labyrinth brighter than they had ever been. The town had installed lamps on many of the street corners. It was, indeed, growing, and soon might not be a place where he could feel safe and at home. He might need to find another small, out of the way town to spend his off-trail hours in.

On his way to his hotel, he passed the barbershop and saw a light. Through the window he could see Melanie, the barber, sweeping her floor. He wondered if she'd had enough customers during the day to make that necessary?

She looked up at that point and their eyes met. She straightened, leaned on her broom, and waved at him to come in. He thought, why not? Approached the door and found it unlocked.

"Heading to or from the saloon?" she asked him.

"From," he said. "To my hotel. The day is catching up with me."

"Are you blaming my hot bath?" she asked.

"Partially," he said, "that and all the miles I've covered over the past few days."

"Then you need to relax," she said.

"That's why I'm heading for my hotel," he said. "To relax in bed."

"You could relax right here," she said, "in my chair."

Clint wasn't sure if she was referring to what he thought she might be referring to. After all, she'd had a much better opportunity that afternoon, when he was in the bathtub.

"Melanie—"

"Of course," she said, setting the broom aside, "we'd have to turn down the lamp . . ." She went to the lamp on the wall and turned it down so that they were in almost total darkness. "Now we can't be seen from outside."

"Melanie—"

"Come on, Mr. Adams," she said, "into the chair. Let me show you how to really relax."

He decided to just go ahead and obey and see what happened next.

Chapter Four

Melanie's intent became immediately obvious as she stood in front of Clint and ran her hands up and down his thighs.

"Just relax," she said, in a low tone, "and let me do the work."

"There's going to be work involved?" he asked.

She smiled, leaned forward and kissed him. He wondered what had changed her mind that afternoon, when she was standing next to his bathtub, looking down at his naked form and adding more hot water. Why not strip down and join him, then?

She ran her hands up over his chest, then down again, this time encountering his gun.

"What are you gonna do about this?" she asked.

"Keep it within reach," he said.

"We can do that," she said. "We can hang it right here, from the chair."

He unbuckled the belt, removed it, and hung it where she said. It was within reach for a perfect draw, if the need arose.

"Now," she said, "this other belt—but first, the boots."

He helped him get his boots off, then they worked together to get his pants and underwear off.

When he was sitting in the chair naked from the waist down, she started to unbutton his shirt while his cock hardened.

By the time she removed his shirt, then stepped back to disrobe herself, his eyes had grown used to the dimness in the room. He could see, very clearly, as her curves came into view. When she was completely naked, she stood stock still for a moment and allowed him to take her in. The dim light probably hid some lines and bulges she didn't want him to see, but the ones he could see inflamed his desire even more. She had large breasts with rounded, full undersides. He couldn't see the color of her nipples, but they were large and hard.

"I've never done this before," he said, as she moved forward and took his cock in one hand.

"Had sex?" she asked, stroking him.

"Had sex in a barber chair," he said.

"Ah," she said, "it's a very special place."

"Is there room?"

"There's plenty," she said. "Just wait and see. But for now . . ."

She ducked her head down, took his penis into her mouth, and began to suck him, slowly at first, then more avidly as he began to moan.

She continued to run her hands and nails over his bare thighs as her head bobbed up and down. And just when he thought he wouldn't be able to hold back any longer, she stopped, tightening her hand around the base of his cock.

"Not yet, Mr. Gunsmith," she said. "I'm in charge of when you fire that final shot."

"Whatever you say," he replied. "You're my barber, and I'm in your chair."

"And in my power," she said, getting to her feet. She climbed up onto him, her knees on either side, and sank down on him, taking his hard cock into her wet pussy.

"See?" she said. "Plenty of room. It's a big chair."

He slid his hands beneath her big butt and held her chair as she started to move up and down on him.

"Oh, yeah," she said, "this chair's perfect for this . . . just perfect."

She started to bounce on him, and the chair barely budged, being bolted to the floor as it was. As she bounced faster and faster, he realized she was right, the chair was just perfect for what they were doing.

She put her hands on his shoulders, let her head drop back as she closed her eyes. Her body shuddered and she gushed, wetting them both, as well as the chair.

"Oh Jesus," she said, biting her lip.

The smell of a woman in heat had never offended Clint, and Melanie was no different. As she began to sweat profusely, the scent of it filled the room, mixed with the smell of her other liquids. The combination only increased both of their excitement.

"Okay, wait, wait," she said, slowing down. He didn't know if she was talking to him, or to herself. "Hold on."

She let his cock pop free of her, then stood on the chair with a foot on either side of him. This put her crotch right in front of his face, and he knew what she wanted now.

"Go ahead," she said, balancing herself as well as she could, "go ahead . . ."

He pressed his face to her wet, fragrant pussy, and wrapped his arms around her so as to steady her and keep her from falling.

When his tongue flicked out to taste her, she gasped and said, "Oh God, yessssss . . ."

He began to lick her, lapping up as much of her nectar as he could, while urging her to produce even more. When he felt the tremors building in her, he gripped her even tighter. Her legs tensed and trembled. Between them they managed to keep her standing, and she gushed again . . .

Chapter Five

When the trembling in her legs stopped, she once again dropped down onto him, and started riding him hard. This time, she took him right to his climax, biting her lip so as not to scream when he exploded inside of her . . .

***

"You see?" she said, while she was getting dressed. "The perfect chair."

"You won't get any argument from me," he said, strapping on his gun.

After she'd buttoned her shirt, she walked to the lamp on the wall and turned it up.

"You know," she said, "I almost got into the bathtub with you this afternoon."

"Really?" he asked. "Why didn't you?"

"I guess I didn't know you well enough," she said, "or how you'd react."

"As opposed to tonight?" he said.

She smiled.

"Well," she said, "I did give you a chance to say no and leave."

"So you did."

"And you didn't."

"No," he said, "I didn't."

He looked at the wet marks they had left on her chair.

"So your future customers—"

"Oh," she said, cutting him off, "I wouldn't let little Billy sit in that. I'll clean the chair thoroughly."

"You seem to be pretty . . . experienced at this," he commented.

"You mean, have I done this before with other men?" she asked. "Does that really matter?"

"Actually, no," he said, "it doesn't."

"I didn't think so," she said, "but the answer is no. Oh, I've thought about it, but I needed the right man to come along. Lucky you."

"Yeah," he said, "lucky me."

"Now how about tomorrow we have a meal together," she suggested, "and we really get to know one another."

"That sounds good to me," he said. "Breakfast or supper?"

"Oh, supper," she said, "definitely."

"I'll come by here after you close," he said.

"Come at seven," she said, "That'll give me time to clean up."

"Seven it is, then," he said. "Thanks for the use of the chair . . . again."

She laughed and he went out the door.

***

In his hotel room he looked at the books he'd brought with him to Labyrinth, thinking he might have time to read them all. He had the ever-present Mark Twain, a Robert Louis Stevenson, and a Dickens.

He had been tired when he left the saloon, so now he was even moreso. The books would have to wait for another night. He went right to bed, the pleasant smell of Melanie Jones still in his nostrils . . .

***

In the morning he rose and washed the smell of the night before off before dressing. Another bath wouldn't have been a bad idea, but it was too soon. If he went back to the barber shop for another, Melanie would think he had something else in mind. He wanted to have that supper with her, first, before they did anything else.

When he'd done the best he could to clean up, he went downstairs to have breakfast with Rick Hartman.

***

"Just in time," Rick said, as Clint entered the saloon. "Shiloh's just finished the eggs."

"How do you keep finding these bartenders who can also cook?" Clint asked, sitting across from his friend.

"It's part of the job," Rick said. "By the way, do you like your hair cut?"

"I do," Clint said. "She's a very good barber."

"Really? I'll have to try her, then," Rick said. "I've been doing it myself."

"I can tell," Clint said, as Shiloh brought out their ham-and-eggs. "Maybe haircuts should also be part of the bartender's job."

"I can do that," Shiloh said.

"Never mind," Rick said. "Making breakfast and tending bar are enough. Thanks, Shiloh."

"I'll bring the coffee out, boss."

"Good man!" Rick leaned forward. "He makes strong coffee."

"He better," Clint said. "I'd expect that to be part of the job, too."

Chapter Six

After breakfast Rick had Shiloh bring two beers to the table.

"Isn't it a little early?" Clint asked.

"For you, maybe," Rick said. "I've been starting earlier and earlier, these days."

"Why?"

"Let's call it the strain of the job."

"Well," Clint said, pushing the beer away, "I'm not feeling that way—not yet, anyway."

"Jesus," Rick said, "if I was you, I'd be jittery all the damn time."

"I used to be," Clint said.

"What happened?"

"I got older," Clint said. "I started realizing the pressure could kill me."

"By . . . what? Making you think too much?"

"Yeah," Clint said, "and at the wrong time."

"You and me," Rick said, "we live different kinds of lives, and deal with different kinds of things. Granted, yours involve life and death, but mine . . . it involves my life, and my livelihood."

"Are you having problems here, with the saloon?" Clint asked.

"Always," Rick said. He finished his beer, put his empty glass down and grabbed Clint's. "But I'm handling it."

Clint studied his friend, noticed lines in his face he hadn't seen the last time he was there—mostly around the eyes, and along his forehead.

"I gotta get to work," Rick said. standing up, "You know, bills to pay."

"Rick," Clint said, "you wouldn't be looking for investors, would you?"

Rick sat back down.

"You?"

"I've got some money floating around."

"That would make us partners," Rick observed.

"So?"

"It would change our relationship," Rick went on. "We're friends now. I want to keep it that way."

Clint thought a moment, then said, "Yeah, okay. I get it."

Rick stood again.

"I'll see you later," he said.

"Tonight," Clint said. "I'll stop in for that beer."

"See you then."

***

Clint understood Rick's reluctance to take money from him. He was right, it would change their relationship. But up to now, Clint had always thought Rick's place was a solid moneymaker. If there was trouble, he hoped Rick would be able to handle it. His friend had always seemed to be solid and in control, but the lines in his face and the early drinking were a concern.

He'd return to Rick's Place later to see if his friend's demeanor had changed.

He spent the rest of the afternoon looking in on Eclipse, making sure the Darley was comfortable and well taken care of. Then he did some work on his saddle, which had a worn cinch that needed replacing. Following that, he broke down his guns—his Peacemaker, rifle and Colt New Line—cleaned them thoroughly, and reassembled them, satisfied that they were all in proper working order.

On his way back to Rick's place for that beer, he passed the barber shop and saw Melanie in the window. Once again, it looked like she was sweeping the floor. He hoped it was because she'd had a lot of customers that morning and afternoon.

He crossed the street, stepped to the window and knocked on it. She looked up and smiled, then beckoned him to come in.

As he entered, she sat her broom aside and put her hands on her hips.

"Back for another haircut?" she asked. "Or just another session in the chair."

"Another session sounds inviting, I can't do supper at seven" he said. "Let's meet later."

"Where?"

"My hotel?"

"Are you inviting me to your room, Mr. Adams?" she asked. "Do you know what that would do to my reputation as a respectable lady?"

"If having sex in your chair in front of this window didn't damage your reputation," he pointed out, "I doubt anything would."

"Good point," she said. "Nine or so?"

"Nine's good," he said. "And if you like, you can sneak up the back stairs."

"I'll give it some thought," she promised, grabbing her broom again.

He left the barber shop and headed for the saloon to check on his friend.

Chapter Seven

For the next few days, Clint kept an eye on Rick during the day, and both eyes—and hands—on Melanie at night—first in his room, then hers, then back again.

After four days of this, they woke up in Clint's room, and had their arms and legs entangled when there was a knock on Clint's door.

"What?" Clint yelled.

"It's Rick. Come on, wake up!"

"I'm awake."

"Then open the damn door!"

Melanie wrapped herself in the bed sheet and said, "Go ahead and open it."

Clint stood up, pulled on his trousers, then walked to the door barefoot. Even though he knew Rick's voice, he still carried his gun with him. You never knew when someone was being forced to do something.

He swung the door open just as his friend was about to knock again.

"Finally!" Rick said.

"What's going on?" Clint asked.

"There's a man over at my place looking for you," Rick said.

"This early? Your place isn't even open."

"Well, he kept beating his fist on the door until I had Shiloh answer it."

"This better be good, Rick."

Rick looked past him into the room, saw Melanie on the bed, wrapped in the sheet.

"It might not be as good as this," he admitted, "but then again . . ."

"Come on, Rick," Clint said. "It's early."

"That's what I told him, but he insisted he wanted to see you right away."

"Who insisted?" Clint asked.

"The man in my saloon."

"What man?" Clint asked, showing his exasperation.

"Well, I didn't believe him at first," Rick said, "but then I thought I should leave it up to you."

"Leave what up to me?" Clint asked. "Jesus, Rick, this is like pulling teeth—"

"Your brother."

Clint hesitated, then asked, "What?"

"There's a man in my saloon," Rick said, "who says he's your brother."

***

Clint sent Rick back to the saloon, said he'd be there as soon as he got dressed.

"You have a brother?" Melanie asked.

He dressed without answering.

"Oh," she said, "it's something you don't wanna talk about?"

"Not until I go to the saloon and see who this is," Clint said.

"So you have a brother, but this might not be him," she said.

He strapped on his gun and headed for the door.

"Will you be coming back?"

"You'd better get yourself some breakfast and then go to work," he replied. "This might take a while."

"The brother who may not be a brother?" she asked, smiling.

"We'll talk about it later," Clint said, and left the room.

***

When Rick got back to the saloon, he saw that Shiloh had given the man some breakfast.

"I hope you don't mind," the man said. "Your bartender must've seen how hungry I was."

"I didn't think you'd mind, boss," Shiloh said.

"Not as long as you get my breakfast ready," Rick said, "and one for Clint."

"Comin' up!" Shiloh promised.

"Then he's coming?" the man asked.

"He is," Rick said. "He'll be here any minute."

The man stared across the table at Rick.

"Did he say anything?"

"About what?" Rick asked.

"About me."

"No, not a thing," Rick said.

The man sat back in his chair and stared at his half-finished breakfast.

"Well," he said, "I don't know what I expected."

"You better finish that breakfast," Rick said. "Shiloh doesn't like when his food goes to waste."

"He's your bartender?"

"He is."

The man picked up his fork.

"He's a very good cook," he said.

"Only in the morning," Rick said.

Chapter Eight

During the walk from the hotel to Rick's Place Clint thought about his family and his life back East. It was a long time ago, and he didn't think very much about it, normally. But this was bringing it all back, and he wasn't grateful for the flood of memories.

He shook his head to dispel the past and decided to simply dwell on the present. He'd find out who this was claiming to be his brother, and deal with it.

When he reached Rick's Place he stopped just in front. He had no idea who was waiting for him inside, but he would keep his gun hand ready for anything.

The front door was open, and he entered.

***

Rick saw Clint come in the front door, but the man seated across from him didn't. If he was the Gunsmith's brother, he certainly had no problem sitting with his back to the door.

Rick decided to simply wait for Clint to reach the table before saying anything.

***

Clint reached the table and looked down at the man seated across from Rick Hartman.

"Hello, Johnny."

The other man looked up, smiled and said, "Hi, Clint."

Rick looked at the two men. Johnny was about ten years younger, and there was no family resemblance that he could see.

"I suppose you two would like to be alone," Rick said.

"Yeah, thanks, Rick."

"Oh," Rick said, surprised. He had hoped to be able to sit in on this reunion. He stood up and picked up his plate.

"Shiloh will bring out some breakfast for you, Clint," he said.

"Thanks."

Rick moved to another table across the room, while Clint claimed the chair his friend had just vacated.

"What're you doing here, Johnny?" Clint asked.

"Lookin' for you," Johnny said. "I heard you came to this town from time to time."

"Who told you that?" Clint asked.

"Who remembers?" Johnny said. "I just headed west, started askin' questions, and this was what I got. Glad to see it was accurate."

Shiloh came out from the kitchen and put a plate and a mug of coffee down in front of Clint.

"What's it been?" Johnny asked. "Twenty years?"

"More like twenty-five," Clint said.

"Doesn't seem possible," the younger man said.

"It does to me."

"You're not still mad, are you?" Johnny asked.

"Only when I think back."

"You know," Johnny said, "I was pretty young when you left. I don't really remember all of it."

"That's okay," Clint said. "It's not worth remembering."

"Pa's gettin' old, you know?" Johnny said. "He'd like to see you."

"Your Pa," Clint said, "not mine."

"Still—"

"Is that what brings you here, Johnny?" Clint asked. "To convince me to come back East?"

"Not exactly," Johnny said, sitting back in his chair. "You see, I haven't been back East in a while, myself. I came west ten years ago, been here ever since."

"Is that right?" Clint Asked. "I hadn't heard about that."

"You haven't heard anything because I don't go around tellin' people the Gunsmith is my brother."

"That's good," Clint said, "but now you're here, claiming to be my brother."

"We *are* brothers," Johnny said.

"We don't have the same father," Clint said.

"But Ma—"

"Johnny," Clint said, "tell me what you want."

"I need your help, Clint."

"With what?"

"A personal matter."

"There's nobody here but you and me," Clint told him.

Johnny looked around. Shiloh was in the back, and Rick was seated across the room, eating his breakfast.

"Rick can't hear us," Clint said, eating his own food. "Just tell me what's going on so we can get it done."

"It's not gonna be that easy," Johnny said.

"Why?"

"Well, it's really somethin' I need to show you, not tell you."

"So you want me to go with you someplace?"

"Yes."

"Why me?"

"Because you're the only one who can help me, Clint," Johnny said. "There's nobody else."

Chapter Nine

Clint told Johnny to get himself a hotel room and they would talk later.

"Tell Mr. Hartman thanks for the breakfast," Johnny said, getting to his feet. "I'll see you later."

Clint nodded, kept eating his breakfast as Johnny left. Rick picked up his plate and carried it over to join Clint.

"So?" he said.

"So?"

"Was it a family reunion?" Rick asked. "Is that fella your brother?"

"It's complicated," Clint said.

"Well, what's he want?"

"He says he needs my help."

"With what?" Rick asked.

"We didn't get that far."

"Why not?"

"Well," Clint said, "mainly because I didn't want to."

"Why not?"

Clint didn't answer.

"Don't tell me, let me guess," Rick said. "It's complicated."

Clint nodded.

Shiloh came out with the coffee pot, and both men held their cups out.

***

Clint knew if he went to the barber shop, he'd have to tell Melanie the same things he had just told Rick—it was complicated. It actually wasn't. Johnny was from Clint's past, a past he had gone to great lengths to put behind him and forget. He had never been a family man, which may have been why he had only come close to marrying once, many years ago. When she died he didn't come close again . . . ever.

He had never expected that anyone from the life he had left behind in the East would show up in the West. He had enough to deal with in his everyday life, and didn't need anything popping up from the past.

Now this.

Whatever help Johnny needed, he would have to get from somewhere else. Clint would listen to his story, then try to steer him to someone else.

***

Clint checked in at his hotel, one of two that Labyrinth had.

"Yes, sir," the clerk said, "he checked in a little while ago."

"Can I see how he signed the register?"

"Sure thing," the clerk said, turning the book around.

Clint ran his finger down the page, came to the name Johnny Adams.

"Hey, I just noticed that," the clerk said. "Is he any relation?"

"Why? Did he say he was?"

"Naw, didn't say a word," the clerk said. "Just that he needed a room, and when I gave him his key he went up."

"My floor?"

"Well, yeah, but all the way at the other end of the hall," the clerk said.

"Good."

"Is there a problem, Mr. Adams?"

"No problem at all," Clint said.

Clint decided to leave the hotel. He didn't want to run into Johnny just yet.

But he did run into Melanie, right out front. So he was going to have to deal with it, after all.

"There you are," she said. "I was just gonna open, but I thought I'd check in with you, first."

"Let's go to your place," Clint said. "I'll need to get comfortable in your chair for this."

***

When they got to the barber shop Melanie unlocked the door so they could get in, then locked it again and left the Closed sign on the door.

Clint got comfortable in her chair.

"You want a trim while we talk?" she asked.

"That's not necessary," he said.

There were some chairs for customers to sit in while they waited their turn. So far, they had never been used, since she opened. She dragged one over and sat in it, facing Clint, who was looking in the mirror.

"Was it your brother?" she asked.

"It was somebody from my past," Clint said. "His name's Johnny."

"Johnny . . . Adams?" she asked.

"That's the name he's using," Clint admitted.

She folded her arms and said, "I guess I'll just have to sit here and wait for you to tell me as much as you need to."

Chapter Ten

"My family's from Philadelphia," Clint said.

"You have family there?"

"I did," he said, giving her a hard look.

"Sorry," she said, raising her hands. "No more questions. I'll just listen."

"There's not much to listen to," Clint said. "When I left, Johnny was about eight or nine. We weren't close, so I don't know why he came looking for me now."

He stopped and she kept silent, even though she had half a dozen questions.

"Look, I wasn't close with anyone in my family, and all I wanted to do back then was leave." He frowned. "I've been thinking it was twenty-five years, but now I see it's been closer to thirty."

"Are you sure it's him?" she asked. "I mean, the same kid, all grown up?"

"No," Clint said, "actually, I'm not sure, at all."

"Sorry," she said, "that was a question."

"And a very good one."

He got out of the chair and headed for the door.

"Where are you goin'?"

"I'm going to see if I can be sure one way or another," he said. "Thanks for the question, Melanie."

He went out the door as she shouted, "You're wel-come!"

***

When Clint got back to the hotel, he walked up to the second floor to the end of the hall and knocked on the door. He had to knock a second time before it was answered by a bleary-eyed Johnny.

"Oh, hey, Clint," he said. "Sorry, but I was out—"

"You mind if I come in?"

"No, come ahead."

Clint went in and Johnny closed the door. As the young man turned to face him Clint looked intently at his face, trying to see the eight-year-old he'd left behind all those years ago.

"You mind if I wash my face to wake up?" Johnny asked.

"No," Clint said, "go ahead."

The younger man stripped off his shirt, poured some water into a basin and proceeded to wash his face and hands. Clint studied the pale skin on the man's back.

As Johnny turned to face Clint, drying his face and hands on a towel, he asked, "Are you ready to talk about my problem?"

"Sure, why not?" Clint said. "But let's go and do it someplace else."

"The saloon?"

"A saloon," Clint corrected.

***

Instead of going back to Rick's Place, Clint took Johnny to a small saloon on the other end of town, called The Deep End.

As they entered, Clint saw the bartender behind the bar, and nobody else in sight.

"Grab a table," Clint said. "I'll get two beers."

"This early?"

"It's late enough," Clint said.

He went to the bar, got two beers from the bored looking bartender, and carried them to the table.

"This place always like this?" Johnny asked.

"Usually."

"Okay, well—"

"Before you tell me your problem," Clint said, "fill me in."

"On what?"

"On everything you've been doing since I last saw you?"

"You want me to go through twenty-five years—"

"It's more like thirty."

"Okay, thirty. That's a lot to go through."

"Just give me the high points."

"Well," Johnny said, "there aren't a lot of those."

"The low points, then."

Johnny sipped his beer and said, "There are plenty of those."

***

The gist was that after Clint left, Johnny's father started drinking even more, took his anger out on Johnny by beating him and his older brothers, Joey and Scott.

"What happened to them?" Clint asked.

"They both left, like you did," Johnny said. "I had to hang around until I was thirteen and could get out of there, too."

"And have you come across them at all?" Clint asked. "Your brothers?"

"No," Johnny said, "not in all this time."

"What have you been doing?" Clint asked.

"This and that. I was a cowhand for a while, I learned how to use a telegraph key, I wrote for a small-town newspaper, I tended bar . . . I've done a lot of different things."

"And you used your real name for all that?" Clint asked.

"I did," he said. "I'm Johnny Adams, and nobody's ever asked me if I was related to the Gunsmith."

"All right," Clint said, "so you've kept a low profile all these years. You might as well tell me what problem has prompted you to look me up."

Johnny took a deep breath and then said, "Somebody wants to kill me."

Chapter Eleven

"Keep talking," Clint said.

"Well," Johnny said, "with all the things I've done over the years, I managed to cross to the wrong side of the law once or twice."

"Ah."

"So I was involved in this bank job—"

"Anybody killed?" Clint interrupted him.

"No," Johnny said, "it wasn't anything like that. It was well thought out and planned."

"By you?"

"No, by a man named Max Quentin."

"Never heard of him."

"That's because his plans are flawless," Johnny said.

"So what happened with this one?"

"It went off without a hitch," Johnny said. "The problem is what happened after."

"Which was?"

"Somebody ran off with the money."

"But not you."

"No, it wasn't me. I swear."

"Then who was it?"

"Another member of the gang," Johnny said.

"Do you know who?"

"No," Johnny said, then, "I swear!"

"Okay, so who thinks it was you?"

"Quentin."

"And he's after you?"

"Oh, yeah," Johnny said. "He's put the word out. This is the only place I've felt safe for months."

"Months," Clint said. "When did this all happen?"

"Last year," Johnny said. "I've been tryin' to find you since then."

Clint sat back in his chair and stared at the younger man.

"Clint," Johnny said, "I'm tellin' you the truth. I mean, I admit I was part of a gang that robbed a bank, but it's the only time I ever did anythin' like that."

"How did you meet Max Quentin?" Clint asked.

"In a saloon," Johnny said. "He and his men were drinkin', and I realize now they were lookin' for some-body. It turned out to be me. I fit whatever they were lookin' for."

"So now you want me to bail you out."

"God, yes!" Johnny said.

"How?"

"Find Max Quentin," Johnny said, "and convince him to leave me alone."

"How do you propose I do that?" Clint asked.

"You're the Gunsmith," Johnny said. "He'll listen to you."

"And if he doesn't?" Clint asked. "Do you want me to kill him?"

"Well," Johnny said, "I guess that'd be up to him."

"No, Johnny," Clint said, "it's up to me. I'm not about to kill someone just to save your neck."

"Clint," Johnny said, "you're my brother."

"Johnny, the last time I saw you, you were eight years old. To be honest, I don't even know if you're that person."

"You can't tell by lookin' at me?" Johnny asked, surprised.

"No, I can't."

Johnny shrugged helplessly and said, "I don't know how I can prove it to you."

"You can't, really," Clint said.

"So then what do I do?" Johnny asked.

"I think you're going to have to convince Max Quentin yourself," Clint said.

"He'll kill me as soon as he sees me," Johnny said.

"Not if he thinks you took the money," Clint said. "First, he'll try to get you to tell him where it is. You better think about that."

Now Johnny looked surprised.

"You think I took it?" he asked.

"I don't know," Clint said. "I don't know you well enough to trust you."

"So you're just gonna let me be tortured, then killed?" Johnny asked.

"I hope that doesn't happen."

"Jesus Christ," Johnny said, "is that all I'm gonna get from you?"

"I'm afraid so," Clint said.

He stood up.

"Do you want me to beg?" Johnny asked. "I mean, I'll do it. I'll beg."

"Don't."

"If I was a stranger, would you help me?"

Clint leaned over and said, "You are a stranger. If I was you, I'd leave town tomorrow and see if I could find Max Quentin. The faster you deal with this, the better chance you'll have of surviving."

"Deal with it? How?"

"Either convince Quentin you didn't take the money," Clint said, "or else find out who did."

Chapter Twelve

When Clint bellied up to the bar at Rick's Place, Shiloh came over and asked, "Beer?"

"Yep."

Clint looked around.

"Is Rick here?" Clint asked, accepting the beer.

"He's in his office," Shiloh said. "Lookin' over some bills."

"Thanks."

"Sure."

Clint carried his beer to the back wall and knocked on the door of Rick's office.

"I'm busy!" Rick snapped from inside. "Handle it yourself!"

Clint opened the door and looked in.

"Is that meant for me?" he asked.

Rick looked up from his desk, then shook his head and waved Clint in.

"No, of course not," he said. "Come on in and have a seat."

Clint entered and sat across the desk from Rick.

"How'd things go with Johnny?" Rick asked.

"Not good," Clint said. "He'll be leaving tomorrow."

"So soon?"

"Not soon enough."

"So, is he your brother?" Rick asked.

"I don't know," Clint said. "I don't think so."

"Do you have a brother?"

Clint hesitated, then sipped his beer.

"After my father died, my mother remarried a man with three sons."

"Ah," Rick said, "so step-brothers."

"They thought so," Clint said. "I never did. I was older, and we never fit together."

"What about your mother?"

"Soon after they got married," Clint said, "she died. After that, I left."

"Why?"

"I had to leave," Clint said, "or kill him."

"Kill who?"

"The man who married my mother."

"Your step-father," Rick said.

"I never thought of him that way," Clint said.

"So as far as you're concerned, no step-father, and no step-brothers."

"No."

"Is that why you haven't agreed to help this fella, Johnny?"

"That, and the fact that he's a bank robber."

"What?"

49

Clint told Rick the story Johnny had told him about Max Quentin and the robbery.

"Max Quentin?" Rick repeated. "I don't know that name."

"I didn't, either," Clint said.

"Does he exist?"

Clint stared at Rick.

"That's a good question," he said. "Do you think he was lying to me, Rick?"

"Actually," Rick said, "I thought he was telling the truth."

"Well," Clint said, "I can't even tell if he's the real Johnny. I mean, the last time I saw him he was a child."

"So you think he was just trying to get the Gunsmith on his side by claiming to be your brother?"

"Yes."

"So you're not going to help him."

"I gave him my best advice," Clint said, "but no, I'm not going to go looking for Max Quentin."

Rick stood up, walked to a sideboard and poured himself a glass of brandy. He didn't offer Clint any because he knew he didn't like it. And besides, he had his beer.

He went back to his desk and sat down.

"You know he'll probably get himself killed," he said to Clint.

"If any of his story is true," Clint added.

"He may not be your step-brother," Rick said, "but I think the whole bank robbery story is true. Why don't you let me check on it? See what I can find out about Max Quentin."

"By tomorrow morning?"

"Let me worry about that," Rick said.

"All right," Clint said. "I'd appreciate it."

"Besides, it'll get me away from this shit?" Rick said, looking down at his desk.

"Bills?"

"Lots of them," Rick said, "but that's my problem. You going to be around for a while?"

"It's early, so yes," Clint said. "I'll just have another beer."

"Well," Rick said, "give me a few hours."

Clint stood up, then gestured to Rick's desk.

"Are you sure I can't help—"

"Yes," Rick said, cutting him off, "I'm sure, Clint. I'll handle it, like I always do."

Clint nodded and left the office.

Chapter Thirteen

Clint went back to the bar and ordered a second beer from Shiloh.

"The boss okay?" the bartender asked, as he delivered the beer.

"He seems to be," Clint said. "He's just a little more stressed than I've ever seen him before."

"Yeah, I noticed that," Shiloh said.

"Do you have any idea what it's about," Clint asked. "I mean, besides bills?"

"Nope," the bartender said. "He don't talk to me about things like that."

"What about his woman?" Clint asked. "Would she know?"

"Maybe," Shiloh admitted, "but I doubt she'd say. Not if she wants to stay his woman."

"Good point."

Shiloh moved on to serve a new customer. Clint held his beer and turned to have a look around. The gaming tables were all full, which was okay with him. He wasn't in the mood to gamble.

He nursed his beer, and another, for two hours, pausing only to eat some hardboiled eggs that Shiloh brought out.

"It's better to have somethin' in your stomach," the bartender said.

"Thanks."

He had finished his eggs, and a third beer, by the time Rick appeared from his office and approached the bar. By the time he got there, Shiloh had a beer waiting for him."

"Thanks, Shiloh."

"Sure thing."

Rick turned to Clint.

"Max Quentin is a bad one," he said.

"I hope you found out more than that," Clint said.

"He robs banks," Rick said. "Apparently, he's got two men he uses each time, but he takes on others for each job."

"That was probably Johnny," Clint said.

"He's killed bank employees before," Rick said. "Managers, tellers, clerks."

"Has he ever robbed a bank without killing anyone?"

"A time or two," Rick said, "but somebody usually dies."

"So Johnny might've lied about that," Clint said. "He said he didn't kill anybody."

"Maybe he didn't," Rick said.

"If Quentin did, or any of his men, then Johnny's just as guilty in the eyes of the law."

"That's a tough way to look at it," Rick said.

"If he was my brother, it would be," Clint agreed.

"So you still don't believe it."

"The kid I knew had a scar on his back," Clint said. "I saw Johnny in his room without his shirt on. No scar. So no, I don't believe him."

"Well," Rick said, "if what you told me is true—and what he told you is true—there's not much doubt that Max Quentin will kill him."

"Then he better avoid Quentin," Clint said, "or find out who really has the money."

"Or, if he has it, give it back."

"Right."

"What are you going to tell 'im?"

"Nothing," Clint said. "I've told him all I can. The rest is up to him."

"So you'll let him ride out in the morning?"

"Let him?" Clint asked. "I'll insist on it."

"You wanna bring the law in on this?" Rick asked.

"Who's the sheriff, these days?"

"A new man—new to this town, that is, not to wearing a badge. His name's Kincaid."

"I don't know him," Clint said, "so no, let's keep him out of it."

"How are you gonna feel if this Johnny gets killed?" Rick asked. "Have you thought about that?"

"Yes," Clint said, "and I've thought about always getting myself involved in other people's troubles. It might be time for me to just worry about myself."

Rick snorted.

"What? You don't think I can do it?"

"No, I don't," Rick said. "Oh, it's not that you're a busybody, but you can't walk away from people in trouble."

"Well," Clint said, "watch me walk away from this one."

Clint finished his beer.

"Thanks for filling me in on Quentin," Clint said. "It confirms my decision for me."

"So you believe Johnny robbed a bank?"

"I do," Clint said, "and I don't get myself involved in the problem of two bank robbers who are fighting over the money."

"What if you could get the money back for the bank?" Rick asked. "And put the bank robbers away?"

"That's for the law to do, Rick," Clint said. "Not me."

"What if there's a reward?"

"Why are you trying to convince me to help him?" Clint asked.

"Because I know you better than you know yourself," Rick said. "If you don't do it, you'll regret it."

"You know," Clint said, "one of the reasons I came here was to spend some time and do some thinking. So why don't you leave me alone and let me think?"

Rick shrugged helplessly and said, "So okay, go and think."

Chapter Fourteen

The man claiming to be Johnny Adams rode out the next morning. He and Clint didn't speak again.

Clint was getting a haircut from Melanie a week later when Sheriff Kincaid came into the shop. They had seen each other in passing while Clint was there but had never spoken. The sheriff knew Clint's history in Labyrinth and was satisfied that the Gunsmith was never there to cause trouble.

"Mr. Adams," Kincaid said.

"Sheriff," Clint said, looking at the bushy gray hair that curled from beneath the man's hat. "Are you in here for a haircut?"

"'fraid not," the lawman said.

"Are you gonna arrest me, Sheriff?" Melanie asked.

"Not at all, Ma'am," the sheriff said. "I'm here to talk to Mr. Adams."

"You can talk to me while she cuts my hair," Clint told him. "What's on your mind?"

"I got a telegram this mornin'."

"And why does that concern me?"

"Because it mentions you."

Clint had been looking at the sheriff in the mirror, but now he turned his head as Melanie stopped cutting his hair and stepped back.

"Mentioned me in what way?"

The sheriff took a telegram from his shirt pocket.

"This is from the sheriff in a town called Headstone, Wyoming."

"Headstone?" Clint asked. "What kind of name is that for a town?"

"All I know is a man claiming to be your brother was killed there. The sheriff wanted me to inform you."

"Sheriff," Clint said, "I don't have a brother."

Kincaid frowned at the telegram.

"Johnny Adams? Is that name familiar?"

"There was a Johnny Adams here a week ago, claiming to be my brother," Clint said. "I wasn't convinced."

"Well," Kincaid said, "A man named Max Quentin is saying he killed the Gunsmith's brother, and you can't do a thing about it."

"Can I see that?" Clint asked.

"Of course."

The sheriff handed the telegram to Clint, who read it and handed it back.

"Sheriff Jenkins, do you know him?" Clint asked.

"Never heard of him or the town."

"Then how did he hear of you in order to send you the telegram?"

"He sent it to the sheriff of Labyrinth, Texas," Kincaid said, "not me, personally."

"So," Clint said, "the only personal touch was my name."

"That's right."

"It came in this morning, you said?"

"Yes."

"So the killing must've happened in the past few days."

"I'd say so."

Clint turned back to the mirror.

"Okay, Sheriff," he said, "you've informed me."

"So what are you gonna do?"

"I'm going to finish my haircut."

"But—"

"Thanks, Sheriff," Clint said.

Kincaid stared at Clint for a few moments, then stuffed the telegram back into his pocket.

"I have to send a reply," he said. "What do you want me to say?"

"Tell 'em you gave me the message."

"And?"

"That's it."

"You don't want me to tell them that you'll be comin'?" Kincaid asked.

"If you tell them that, Sheriff," Clint said, "then they'll know I'm coming."

Kincaid stared at him a moment longer, and when Clint didn't look away from the mirror, and didn't say another word, the lawman left.

Melanie began cutting Clint's hair, again.

"What do you intend to do?" she asked.

"Tomorrow I'll leave and head for the town of Headstone," Clint said.

"But they'll be expectin' you, won't they?"

"Maybe not," Clint said. "Not if they don't hear from Kincaid that I'm coming."

"But why are you goin'?" she asked. "You said Johnny wasn't your brother."

"Well, one," Clint said, "I don't know that the Johnny who was here is the Johnny who was killed in Headstone."

"Ah," she said, "and two?"

"Two, if I do nothing, then Max Quentin will keep spreading the word that he killed the Gunsmith's brother, and I did nothing about it."

"So?"

"So that would paint an even bigger target on my back than I have on a normal day."

"But you're gonna go, anyway?"

"Yes," Clint said. "I have an appointment with a man named Max Quentin."

Chapter Fifteen

Clint got Eclipse ready to leave the next morning, then rode him over to Rick's Place to have breakfast with Rick one last time before leaving.

"Ready to go?" Rick asked, as Clint entered.

"Just need one more of Shiloh's breakfasts to hold me for a while," Clint said, seating himself.

At that moment, the bartender came out with two plates and set them down on the table.

"What are your plans?" Rick asked, as they ate.

"Well, first I'll have to find out if the Johnny Adams who was killed in Headstone is the same one who was here," Clint said. "Then I'll see if the sheriff there has any idea where Max Quentin is."

"So you intend to take this up with Quentin, after all," Rick said.

"Not for revenge," Clint pointed out, "and not to get the bank's money back. This is to protect my good name, and not have even more young guns coming out of the woodwork to take pot shots at me."

"What about somebody to watch your back in Headstone?" Rick asked.

"Are you volunteering?" Clint asked.

Rick laughed.

"You know I can't hit the side of a barn with a gun, Clint," Rick said, "or I would. You need somebody who can handle themselves."

"Well, I'll wait until I get there and assess the situation," Clint said. "I'll talk with Sheriff Jenkins and see what's what."

"I wish you luck," Rick said. "And I'll tell you something. I hope for your sake that you don't find the dead man is a member of your family, in some way."

"I left family behind a long time ago, Rick," Clint said. "I did that the first time my mother's husband put his hands on her."

"He beat her?"

"He did it once, and that was all she took. But she died shortly after that, and I decided to come out here and leave that all behind me."

"I never knew that."

"Nobody ever did," Clint said. "It's not something I talk about. And it's probably something I'll never talk about, again."

They finished their breakfasts, and then both stood and shook hands.

"I wish you luck," Rick said, "and we'll see you back here, soon."

"I'll be back."

"But remember one thing."

"What's that?" Clint asked.

"If you need my help, whether I can handle a gun or not, you just send me a telegram," Rick said, "and I'll be there."

"I know you will."

Clint turned, left the saloon, mounted Eclipse and rode over to the barber shop.

***

They had not spent the night together, because it was Clint's last night before heading out. Melanie said it was too sad, but she asked him to stop by her shop before he left, to say goodbye.

She was in her shop, but had the CLOSED sign on the door. She didn't want to be with a customer when Clint came over. So, she sat in the chair and stared out the window, and when she saw him ride up on that majestic Darley Arabian, she stood up and unlocked the door.

***

Clint dismounted and, as she reached the door with the CLOSED sign on it, Melanie swung it open and stood in the doorway.

"You're ready to go," she said.

"I am."

"You know," she said, "the way my business is goin', I may not be here when you get back."

"I know that."

"So this is probably goodbye."

"Melanie—"

"I know, I know," she said. "We didn't make any promises to each other, and you're not the kind of man who's gonna settle down. I know all that. I just ask two things."

"What's that?"

"Make sure you keep your hair lookin' right."

Clint smiled at that and said, "Oh, I will, although I'll probably never have a better barber. And what's the second thing?"

"The second thing," she said, "is . . . just don't go and get yourself killed."

"I'll do my best."

She stood in the doorway, arms folded, as he mounted up and rode out. Then she closed her door, but turned the OPEN sign to face out.

Chapter Sixteen

When Clint Adams rode down the main street of Headstone, Wyoming it had been weeks since he left Labyrinth, Tx. Part of the trip had been by train, but most of it was just he and Eclipse. There was actually no rush to get there, since Johnny Adams—whoever he was— would be a long time buried by the time Clint got there.

So he rode down the street slowly, looking it over as the town did the same to him. Men and women both watched him ride by, curiously. He didn't know if this was usual with every stranger, or only started happening since the shooting of "the Gunsmith's brother."

He noticed that while there were quite a few people on both sides of the street going in and coming out of the businesses, many of them were also simply standing around, looking and pointing.

He decided not to waste any time and ride directly to the sheriff's office. It wasn't hard to find, since it was right on main street, with a large shingle hanging out that said SHERIFF.

He reined in Eclipse in front and just draped his reins over the hitching post.

As he entered the office, a fortyish man wearing a badge looked up from his desk. He had long flowing hair and a flamboyant moustache that must have needed a lot of attention. He wondered what Melanie the barber would have done with it. Clint thought the hair and moustache had looked a lot better on his friend Jim Hickok years before.

"Can I help you?" the man asked.

"You can if you're Sheriff Jenkins."

"That I am," Jenkins said. "And who might you be?"

"The name's Clint Adams."

"Really?" Jenkins frowned and studied Clint.

"Why is that hard to believe?"

"You don't look a thing like your brother."

"Maybe that's because he probably wasn't my brother," Clint said.

"Really?" Jenkins asked. "The town fathers ain't gonna be too happy to hear that."

"So that's why there are so many people on the street?" Clint asked. "Because this is the town where the Gunsmith's brother was killed?"

"Or so we thought," Jenkins said. "A lot of our merchants are gonna be disappointed, too, if you say he wasn't your brother."

"Well, why don't you tell me what happened?" Clint asked. "Then we can go from there."

"Well," Jenkins said, sitting back in his chair, "my best guess is that your brother—uh, the dead man—

must've pulled a bank job with Max Quentin, and then they had a falling out. As a result, Quentin killed him."

"Where?"

"Right out there on the street."

"Gunned him down?"

"Yeah."

"And you didn't arrest him after?"

Jenkins spread his hands in a helpless gesture.

"It was a fair fight," the lawman said. "Everybody saw it."

"And did your local newspaper write about it?"

"Of course."

"And then people started flocking to Headstone," Clint said. "Where'd that name come from, anyway? Who calls a town Headstone?"

"We used to be called Belden, if you can believe it, but ten years ago we got a new mayor and the first thing he did was change the town's name to Headstone. He thought it had more character."

"And now, with the shooting of the Gunsmith's brother . . ."

"Well, yeah," Jenkins said. "Some of us ain't too proud of that."

"You?"

"That's why I sent the telegram to your sheriff," Jenkins said. "I figured you'd wanna know."

"And do something about it."

"Maybe."

"Or maybe you just wanted me to come here and add to the story."

"If you don't want to tell people who you are while you're here, that's fine with me," Jenkins said.

"If you can tell me where Max Quentin is, I'll ride out right now, and you won't see me again."

"Quentin rode out right after the shootin'," Jenkins said. "I don't know where he went, or where he is. Sorry."

"Guess I'll stick around a while, then," Clint said. "Ask some questions."

"You know if you do that, people will figure out who you are," the lawman pointed out.

"I'm sure that just upsets you all to hell," Clint said, and left the office.

Chapter Seventeen

Clint put Eclipse in a livery and himself into a hotel, then went looking for the undertaker. He found him by spotting empty coffins outside, put on display for sale.

He mounted the boardwalk and looked at the coffins. The one to the right of the door was simple, and cheap. The one on the left was more ornate, and expensive.

"Which one do you like, sir?" a man asked, coming out the door.

Most undertakers looked like undertakers—tall, pale, thin, because they didn't spend all that much time with anything but bodies and coffins. This one, however, looked more like a bank manager. He had a rotund stomach, wire-framed glasses and wore a three piece suit.

"What's your name?" Clint asked.

"I'm Henry Oswald, the undertaker. This is my establishment. Have you lost a loved one? Or are you looking for yourself?"

"I'm here about a man who was killed in the street several weeks ago."

The man's eyebrows shot up and he looked happy.

"Johnny Adams? You're his brother, the Gunsmith?"

"I'm Clint Adams," Clint said, "but I doubt he was my brother."

"What?" Now Oswald looked concerned. "But how—"

"Let's go inside and talk about it," Clint suggested.

"Of course, of course," Oswald said. "Come inside."

Oswald led the way. The interior was filled with coffins, and there was hammering from the back.

"That's Ted," Oswald said. "He builds my coffins."

"You don't do that?"

"I design them," Oswald said, "but he makes 'em. Come over here, to my office."

They entered a room that had a desk, two chairs, and no coffins.

"Have a seat, Mr. Adams," the undertaker said, "and tell me what I can do for you."

Clint sat across the desk from the man and took off his hat.

"Tell me about the dead man," he said.

"Your brother—"

"Let's leave that alone," Clint said, cutting him off. "Just tell me about him."

"Well, he was tall, slim, in his thirties," Oswald said. "Quentin shot him twice in the chest, here and here." The undertaker touched the two spots. "Doc says either one would've been enough to kill him."

"This doc, is he still in town?"

"Yeah, he's got an office here," Oswald said.

"I'll go and talk to him later," Clint said. "Can you tell me anything else?"

"Not much," the undertaker said. "I didn't know the fella when he was alive. All I did was bury 'im."

"What about his belongings?"

"Yeah, I got those, but if you're not his brother—"

"Anybody else ask for them?"

"Nope," Oswald said, standing up. "I'll get 'em."

Clint waited while Oswald left the room, wondering if the dead man was the one who had come to seek his help in Labyrinth.

When the undertaker returned, he was carrying a box, but it looked mostly empty.

"This is what he had on him," the man said, placing the box on the table. "I don't know what the hotel did with whatever he had in his room."

Clint stood and looked into the box. There was a gun, a gunbelt, four bits, the clothes he'd been wearing when he was shot.

"There was more than four bits, but I took what I had coming for buryin' him," Oswald said. "I can show you the bill if you—"

"That's fine," Clint said, "I'm sure you took what you had coming."

Clint left everything in the box. He'd been hoping for some kind of letter.

"You can dispose of these things," Clint said. "Keep the four bits, and sell the gun, if you like."

"Yes, sir."

Clint remained standing.

"What's the doctor's name?"

"Doctor Keene," Oswald said. "He has an office over the hardware store down the street."

"Much obliged, Mr. Oswald."

"Uh, sir . . ."

"Yes?"

"The grave has a marker, but no headstone," Oswald said. "Would you like to take care of that?"

"As I said," Clint replied, "there's very little chance that the man was my brother. A marker will do."

"Yes, sir."

Oswald walked Clint to the door, where the two men shook hands and parted.

Chapter Eighteen

Clint stopped in front of the hardware store and looked up at the second floor window. There was a sign there that read M. KEENE, M.D. He walked around to the side and found the stairs leading up. He climbed and knocked on the door. The man who answered was small, wizened, shuffled his feet when he walked. Clint couldn't imagine how the man got up and down the stairway.

"Dr. Keene?"

"That's right." The man stared up at Clint with his grey eyes, frowning. "Are you ill, young man?"

"No, sir," Clint said. "But I do need to talk to you."

"Come in, then," Keene said. "I am available, at the moment."

Keene backed up, and Clint entered.

The room was dark, had a small desk and a second chair.

"Care to sit?" Keene asked.

"That's okay, I can stand."

"Do you mind if I sit?" Keene asked. "My legs aren't what they used to be."

"No, go ahead."

Keene sat heavily at his desk, which faced a wall. The chair was on wheels, and swiveled. He turned around to face Clint.

"There," he said. "What's your name, young man?"

"Clint Adams."

"Ah," Keene said, "you're here about the man who was killed several weeks ago."

"That's right."

"You're brother?"

"Probably not."

"Ah."

"What can you tell me about him?"

"He was shot twice in the chest," Keene said. "Either wound would've been enough to kill him. There was nothing I could do for him."

"Anything else?"

"Like what?"

"Old wounds, scars, any marks . . ."

"No old wounds," Keene said, "but there was some scarring on his back."

"What kind?"

"I had the impression he'd been beaten as a child."

Clint frowned. The man who had come to see him in Labyrinth had no such marks on his back.

"Does that trigger a memory in you?" Keene asked.

Clint didn't answer. Instead he asked, "And did you know the man who killed him?"

"No," Keene said, "but they say it was a bank robber named Max Quentin."

"And you never met him?"

"Never met 'im, never saw 'im," Keene said.

"And you'd have no idea where he went."

"None," the doctor said. "How would I?"

"Okay. Thanks for your time, Doctor."

"Sure," Keene said, "any time. You know, the town has been cashing in on this fella being the brother of the Gunsmith."

"So I've heard."

"Are you going to take that away from us?" Keene asked.

"I don't know," Clint said. "We'll have to see. Thanks again."

Clint left the doctor's office, and as he reached the bottom of the steps, his stomach started to growl. He saw a café across the street and went there for lunch.

***

After lunch Clint found a saloon called PASEO SALOON and had a beer at the mostly deserted bar. There was another man standing at the other end, and a couple of tables, one occupied by a single man, the other by two.

"Ain't seen you in here before," the bartender said.

"That's because I just got to town."

"Why?"

"What do you mean?"

"Why would you come to this town?" the bartender asked. "You ain't interested in that Gunsmith's brother bunk, are ya?"

"Well, actually, I am," Clint said.

"A fella like you?" the bartender asked. "Why?"

"Because my name's Clint Adams."

The barkeep stood up straight. He was about six-four, but had been slouching since Clint entered. In his forties, his hair was thinning on top, and he had a wispy moustache.

"You're the Gunsmith?"

"That's right."

"Well," the bartender said, "I'm really sorry about your brother."

"I'm not sure the dead man was my brother," Clint said.

"Well, he said he was."

"To you?" Clint asked. "He told you?"

"Yeah, he was in here one day, havin' a beer, and he tol' me."

"What's your name?"

"Logan."

"Well, Logan," Clint said, "can you tell me anything else about my so-called brother?"

Chapter Nineteen

"He didn't walk in and start braggin' about bein' your brother, but it did come up a time or two. And then Max Quentin came to town."

"Did you know him when he rode in?"

"Who? Quentin? Well, sort of. He had his crew with him, which was sort of a giveaway."

"So Quentin walked in and started bragging?"

"Not so much," Logan said, "but his men did."

"And did Johnny and Quentin meet in here?" Clint asked.

"I don't know where they met," Logan said, "but Quentin found him in here."

"Found him as if, he was looking for him in the first place?"

"Obviously, because when he saw him in here, he yelled, 'I found you. Did you think I wouldn't?'"

"But he didn't shoot him in here."

"No."

"I wonder why?"

Logan brought a shotgun out from beneath the bar, but the way he was holding it showed he wasn't intending to use it. He simply slapped it down on top of the bar.

"This is why," he said. "I don't allow shootin' in my saloon."

"That's good to know," Clint said. "So they went outside and did it?"

"Not that night, but the next day they were on the street and people were watchin'."

"Were you?"

"I've seen enough gunfights in my time," Logan said. "I didn't need to see a man die in the street."

"Was there any doubt about who would do the dying?"

"Not to me."

"How could you tell?"

"Like I said, "Logan answered, "I've seen a lot of gunfights, and a lot of gunfighters. That Johnny, he was no gunfighter."

"Then what was he doing in the street?"

"He didn't have a choice," Logan said. "You know that better than anybody. A man like Max Quentin doesn't ask you to meet him in the street."

"So he told Johnny to meet him."

"Yep."

"And people heard."

"Everybody knew," Logan said.

"But Johnny came to town before Quentin, right?"

"Yeah, he did," Logan said.

"Did he know anybody here?"

"In here, or in town?"

"In town."

"I don't know that," Logan said, "but he came in here with a couple of guys once or twice."

"Okay then," Clint said, "who were the two guys? Are they still here?"

"Yeah, they're locals," Logan said. "Benny Taylor has a shop at the end of town, where he builds furniture for people. And Ollie Johansen works for him."

"Taylor and Johansen," Clint said, "right. Which end of town would that be?"

"North end," Logan said. "You can't miss it. You'll hear the hammerin'."

"Thanks."

"Come on back when you're done," Logan said. "There are two other saloons in town, but mine's the best."

"I'll keep that in mind," Clint promised.

He left the Paseo Saloon and started walking toward the north end of town.

***

Clint heard the hammering even before he came within sight of the shop. As he approached, he realized it was coming from behind the large, wooden, barn-like building, not from inside. So he walked around to the back to take a look.

He saw a bare-chested man, sweat gleaming on his back, banging on something with a hammer.

"Excuse me," he said, but he had to repeat it again, more loudly this time, for the man to turn.

"Oh, I'm sorry," he said, in a slight Swedish accent, "I couldn't hear you. Can I help you?"

Clint noticed the man was raw-boned, in his forties, powerful looking even though some of the skin sagged from his bones.

"Johansen?" Clint asked.

"That's right," the man said, "Ollie Johansen." He put his hammer down, picked up a rag and began to wipe his chest, arms and face. It wasn't very hot out, but he had been exerting himself.

"I understand you were friends with a man who called himself Johnny Adams."

"Johnny," Johansen said, "Yah, he died a few weeks ago. We were friends."

"He didn't just die, Mr. Johansen," Clint said, "he was killed."

"Come inside," Johansen said. "I can use some cold lemonade."

Clint followed him into the building.

Chapter Twenty

Inside Clint saw that while the exterior made it look like two stories, it was actually one, with very high ceilings, from which hung furniture of all sizes and shapes.

"Hangin' them from the ceilin' makes them dry more evenly after we've painted them."

"Where's your partner?" Clint asked. "Mr. Taylor?"

"Benny has some things to do in town," Johansen said. "He'll be back. You want some lemonade?"

"No thanks, but you go ahead."

Johansen walked to an icy pitcher and poured himself a drink.

"Whataya wanna know?" he asked.

"You and Benny Taylor made friends with a fellow named Johnny Adams when he came to town."

"We did," Johansen said, "but it was a friendship that didn't last long. He got himself killed."

"Yes, I know, by Max Quentin," Clint said.

"The bank robber," Johansen added.

"Did Johnny tell you anything about him and Quentin?" Clint asked.

"Just that a man named Quentin was looking for him," Johansen said.

"Where did you meet him?"

"In the Paseo Saloon."

"And was he asking you for help?"

"No," Johansen said, "we're furniture makers, how could we help him against a bank robber."

"Then why did you become friendly?"

"He bought us drinks," Johansen said. "He was just bein' friendly."

That didn't make sense to Clint. The dead man wouldn't have needed friends. What he needed was help from somebody who could stand with him against Quentin and his men.

"Anything else?" Johansen asked. "I have to get back to work."

"I'd like to talk to your partner."

"He can't tell you anything I didn't tell you," Johansen said, "but I'll let him know you would like to talk to him. Where are you staying?"

"You know," Clint said, "I stopped in the first hotel I came to after the livery. I'm not even sure I remember the name."

"You mean the livery at the end of Main Street?" Johansen asked.

"Yes."

"Then you probably checked yourself into the Claremont Hotel," the carpenter said. "I'll have him look for you there, first."

"What's he look like, so I'll know him?"

"You won't be able to miss him," Johansen said. "He's got red hair and a red beard."

"Okay," Clint said. "Thanks for your time."

***

Clint headed back to a more populated part of town, wondering what the hell he was going to be able to find out about Max Quentin when nobody seemed to know him?

All he knew was that Quentin caught up to "Johnny Adams" here in Headstone and killed him. He didn't know if it was the same Johnny Adams who had come to see him in Labyrinth. Given what Doctor Keene had told him, they probably weren't one and the same.

But why would someone come to him claiming to be Johnny Adams?

He decided to head back to the Paseo Saloon when he saw Sheriff Jenkins coming up the street toward him.

"Are you looking for me?" he asked, as the lawman reached him.

"Sort of," Jenkins said. "I'm makin' my rounds, but I thought if I saw you, I'd find out how you were doin'? Talk to anybody?"

"I talked to Keene, and the bartender at the Paseo Saloon," Clint said. "That led me to a couple of men named Johansen and Taylor."

"The furniture makers?"

Clint nodded.

"Seems Johnny Adams made friends with them while he was here."

"Did they have anythin' to add?" Jenkins asked.

"I spoke to Johansen and he had nothing. I still need to talk to Taylor."

"He won't be hard to find, with that fiery red hair and beard," the lawman told him.

"That's what his partner said."

"So where are you headed now?" the sheriff asked.

"The Paseo Saloon," Clint said. "If your rounds take you by there, I'll buy you a beer."

"I'll be there shortly," Jenkins said, "and I'll take you up on that offer."

Chapter Twenty-One

While Clint was working on a beer in the Paseo, keeping an eye out for Sheriff Jenkins, a man entered, sporting fiery red hair and a bushy red beard.

"You Adams?" he asked, approaching Clint.

"How'd you know?" Clint asked.

"Johansen described you."

"He described you, too."

"Yeah, well, I also know everybody else in here," Taylor said, "so it had to be you."

"Buy you a beer?" Clint asked.

"Only if you want me to talk to you."

Clint waved to Logan the bartender as Taylor bellied up next to him, dwarfing him. The man had to be six-and-a-half feet tall.

"Johansen said you wanna talk about Johnny Adams," Taylor said, after a healthy swallow. "Your brother?"

"It's not for sure he was my brother," Clint said. "What did he tell you?"

"Well, he said you was his brother, all right," Taylor said, "even though you hadn't seen each other in about thirty years."

That sounded about right.

"He didn't offer any further proof?" Clint asked.

"We didn't ask for any," Taylor said.

"Why not?"

"Well," the big man said, with a shrug, "to tell you the truth, we didn't care who his brother was. He was buyin' the drinks, like you are now. So at least you two had that in common."

"Did you see Max Quentin while he was in town?" Clint asked.

"The bank robber who killed Johnny?" Taylor said. "Oh yeah, I seen him. Didn't talk to him, though. He always had some men around him."

"Even on the street," Clint asked, "During the shooting?"

"No, there he was alone—but they was there, watching," Taylor said. "I think if Johnny woulda killed Quentin, they woulda killed him."

"That's good to know."

"You gonna go lookin' for Quentin?"

"I suppose I am."

"For revenge?"

"No," Clint said, shaking his head, "just to get some things straight."

"Like whether or not Johnny was your brother?" Taylor asked.

"I don't think he was," Clint said, "but yes, something like that. Do you have any ideas where Quentin might have gone from here?"

"Not a clue," Taylor said.

"Do you think anybody in town knows?"

"Nobody in town knew 'im," Taylor said. "In fact, we wondered why, after he killed Johnny, he didn't just rob the bank."

"He probably didn't have time to plan it properly," Clint pointed out. "I've heard he plans every job down to the last detail."

"So then he's either off plannin' his next job," Taylor said, "or he's already pullin' it. Why don't you just stand pat and wait to hear?"

"I might have to do just that, Mr. Taylor."

"Buy me another beer and you can call me Benny."

"Logan," Clint called, "give Benny here another beer, on me."

"Comin' up!" Logan said.

Taylor had his fresh beer in hand when Sheriff Jenkins came through the batwing doors.

"He comin' ta drink with you?" Taylor asked.

"I offered to buy him one, yeah."

"Then I'll move on."

"Problems?"

"Me and Jenkins don't get along," Taylor said. "Let's jus' leave it at that."

Taylor took his beer and moved toward the far end of the bar.

"Mr. Adams," Jenkins said, taking up the spot Taylor had vacated.

"Are you ready for that beer now, Sheriff?" Clint asked the lawman.

"As I'll ever be."

Clint waved to Logan again, and the man brought a fresh one over.

"I saw you talkin' with Benny Taylor," Jenkins said.

"Yeah, but he wasn't more helpful than his partner, Johansen," Clint said. "But he did tell me that you and he don't get along."

"He's right about that," Jenkins said.

"What's the problem between you two?" Clint asked.

"I don't rightly know," Jenkins said. "Ain't you ever met a fella you just don't like, and you ain't sure why?"

"One or two, maybe," Clint said, "but I usually have a reason to dislike somebody."

"Well, so do I, but that big fella and his partner, they jus' plain rub me the wrong way, and I can't put my finger on the reason why."

"Ever arrested them?"

"No," Jenkins said, "neither of them has ever seen the inside of my jail."

"Well, good for them."

"So what will you do now, Mr. Adams?"

"I can't even track Quentin, since the trail has surely gone cold," Clint said. "I'm just going to have to keep my ears open from now on, and when I finally hear that he's struck again, I'll have someplace to start."

"So you'll be leavin' town?"

"First thing tomorrow," Clint said. "There's no point in staying here."

"I gotta say I ain't sorry to see you go," Jenkins said. "The longer you stay here, the more chance there is of trouble. Uh, through no fault of yours, of course."

"Of course," Clint said. "I understand, Sheriff," He finished his beer. "I'm going to turn in and get an early start."

"Headin' where?"

"Who knows?" Clint asked. "I'll just give my horse his head, for now."

"Until you hear that Max Quentin and his gang have hit another bank."

"Yes," Clint said, "and they're bound to, sooner or later."

"Well, I wish you luck, then," Jenkins said. "And I hope you discover that the dead man ain't your brother, after all."

"I don't have any brothers," Clint said. "Not real ones, anyway. But I'll need for Max Quentin to stop bragging that he killed the Gunsmith's brother."

"And you can do that by killin' him," the sheriff said.

"Or by putting him away," Clint said.

"Seems to me if you put him in jail, he can still make the claim," Jenkins said. "No, you're gonna have to kill 'im to shut him up."

"I suppose we'll just have to see," Clint said.

***

In the morning Clint checked out, saddled up and rode to Headstone's boot hill before leaving town.

He dismounted and walked to the simple marker that said JOHN ADAMS.

"Whoever you really were," Clint said, to the grave, "I guess it's going to be up to me to see that you get some justice."

He walked back down to Eclipse, mounted up and rode out of Headstone.

Chapter Twenty-Two

It was weeks of drifting before Clint finally heard something about Max Quentin and his gang.

He did some research along the way, stopping in towns to look over their newspaper morgues. It seemed Max Quentin spread himself around, not sticking to one area with his robberies. He had hit banks in every part of the North-and-Southwest. He was apparently trying to make a name for himself as the greatest bank robber of all times. And he stuck to banks. There were no stories about him robbing trains or stagecoaches, or express offices.

Clint was in Denver, Colorado, visiting his friend Talbot Roper when the story of Quentin's latest escapade hit the newspaper.

As Talbot Roper joined him for breakfast in the Denver House Hotel, the detective dropped a copy of the *Rocky Mountain News* onto the table.

"Looks like your guy finally surfaced," he told Clint.

Clint picked up the newspaper and saw the story on page four, which Tal Roper had folded the paper to.

"Quentin gang hits Wyoming bank," he read, aloud. "Kills two."

"Tellers?" Roper asked.

Clint read, then said, "A teller, and then a lawman."

"There'll be a posse after him," Roper said. "They might get him well before you."

"I'll give it a try, anyway," Clint said. "You haven't read this?"

"No," Roper said, looking at the menu, "I figured you'd read it, and give me the highlights. Where did it take place?"

Clint read, again.

"Looks like it was in Rock Springs.

"That's near Green River," Roper said, "about three hundred miles northwest of here."

"How do you know that?"

"I had a case in Green River, recently," Roper said. "Take you about a week to get there. By that time, they may catch Quentin."

"I doubt it," Clint said. "He's been at this a long time. I don't think any posse will run him down."

"But you will, huh?"

"That's right," Clint said, "I will . . ." He picked up a menu. ". . . but not til after breakfast."

Chapter Twenty-Three

A week later, Clint rode into Rock Springs. A sign-post he had passed some time before indicated that Green River was another twenty miles. He knew Green River was a larger town and would have a bigger bank. He wondered why Quentin chose this town's bank.

Rock Springs was a growing town, which might have explained Quentin's choice. A town that was building itself up often had money in its bank. He decided to stop at the sheriff's office first and see what he could find out. With the right information he might be able to leave town again, right away.

In front of the sheriff's office he dismounted, dropped Eclipse's reins to the ground. The horse would remain there until he came back.

He entered the sheriff's office, found a young deputy seated behind the desk.

"I'm looking for your sheriff," Clint said.

"He ain't here."

"Where is he?"

"He and the posse rode out after those bank robbers over a week ago, and they ain't been back, yet."

"Leaving you in charge?"

"Yessir." The young man fidgeted in his chair. "Although, I don't think the sheriff planned on bein' gone this long."

"How big a posse?"

"About ten men."

"How many bank robbers?"

"Five or six."

"But you're thinking the posse may have caught up to the bank robbers and regretted it."

"Mebbe. Can I help you with somethin'?"

"I've been looking for Max Quentin," Clint said. "When I read he hit your bank, I came straight here. This is the closest I've been. Can you tell me which way they went when they rode out of town?"

"West," the deputy said. "The trail ain't gonna be too hard to see, what with the posse takin' off after them. They may have even headed for Green River, but that's only twenty-two miles away. We woulda heard somethin', by now."

"That's true," Clint said. "How much money did the robbers get?"

"Bank manager said about thirty thousand," the deputy answered.

"That much."

"A payroll had just come in," the young man said.

"Seems like Quentin might've known that."

"That's what the sheriff thought."

"Who is your sheriff?" Clint asked.

"His name's Jack Tatum."

"Is he an experienced man?"

"Yeah, some," the deputy said. "He's worn a badge a long time."

"How long in this town?"

"Rock Springs hired him a year ago, but he's worn a badge in other towns."

"So he wasn't elected?"

"Nope," the man said, "he was appointed."

"Okay, thanks." Clint turned to leave.

"Hey," the deputy said, "who are you?"

Clint turned back, his hand on the door knob.

"Clint Adams."

The young man's eyes widened.

"The Gunsmith? And you're gonna track the robbers?"

"I'm going to try."

"Gee, Mr. Adams," the young man said, standing, "can I come with you?"

"You were left in charge here, Deputy," Clint said. "You better just keep doing your job."

The deputy's shoulders slumped.

"I guess you're right." He sat back down.

"What's your name?"

"Todd Wilson."

"If I find your sheriff, Todd," Clint said, "I'll tell him you're doing a fine job."

"Hey, gee, thanks," the deputy said. "I hope you do find 'im."

"I hope so, too," Clint said.

He left the sheriff's office, and Rock Springs, heading toward Green River.

***

What Todd had said about the trail was true. Whether or not he could see the tracks left by the bank robbers, he could certainly see the ones left by the posse. He was able to follow it, and immediately saw that they weren't heading for Green River. The bank robbers and the posse both were bypassing that town. He wondered if the gang had someplace in mind, that they were running to?

"Okay, boy, let's go," he said, to Eclipse, patting the big Darley's neck, "we've got some tracking to do."

Chapter Twenty-Four

When Clint saw the campfire smoke up ahead of him, he knew it wasn't the bank robbers. He reached the camp just as the light was going. What was left of the posse hurriedly got to their feet.

"Stop right there," a man with his arm in a sling said.

"No problem," Clint said. "You the posse from Rock Springs?"

"That's right."

Clint had a feeling the man's sling was hiding his badge.

"Are you Sheriff Jack Tatum?" Clint asked.

"That's right." The sheriff frowned. "You know me?"

"I know your deputy," Clint said.

"Deputy?"

"A boy named Todd?"

"Oh, yeah," Tatum said. "I had to leave that kid in charge. He doin' okay?"

"He's doing fine."

"He send you after us?"

"Nope, I came on my own," Clint said. "I'm looking for Max Quentin."

"So are we," Tatum said.

"Well," Clint said, "it looks like you found him and didn't fare too well."

Clint looked around, saw two or three other men with bandages and slings.

"I heard you left Rock Springs with a dozen men," Clint said, "Looks like you got five or six left."

"Yeah, we caught up to them, all right," the sheriff admitted.

"They took us apart," another man said.

"Shut up, Gene."

"We ain't lawmen," the man called Gene said. "We're storekeepers."

"You're a posse," Sheriff Tatum said. "And you'll act like one."

"We're a busted posse, Sheriff," Gene said. "We got nothin' left."

"You should let them go home, Sheriff," Clint said. "Go on with them."

"And let that gang get away with robbery and murder?" Tatum asked. "They killed the only real deputy I had. I'm not goin' back without them."

"Okay, then," Clint said. "You and me, we'll track them and bring them back. But let these men go home. You've already lost enough."

"What makes you think you and me can do somethin' a twelve-man posse couldn't do?" Tatum asked.

"If you let me dismount and give me a cup of coffee," Clint said, "maybe I'll tell you."

The sheriff thought it over, then lowered his rifle.

"Before you dismount," he said, "what's your name?"

"Clint Adams."

The lawman gave him an exasperated look and asked, "Well, why didn't you say so?"

***

The sheriff sat around the fire with Clint, both of them drinking coffee. The other members of the posse sat around moaning and licking their wounds.

"These men have been harassin' me, tryin' to let me send 'em home," he admitted.

"Well, they don't look like they're going to do you any good in their present state."

"They didn't do me much good when they were healthy," Sheriff Tatum said.

"Then why'd you bring them?" Clint asked.

"I had to get a posse together fast," the sheriff said.

"Well," Clint said, "I suggest you send these men home tomorrow. Keep them out here any longer and they'll not only get killed, they'll get you killed."

"I'll do that," Tatum, said, "now that I got you here as a deputy."

"I'm not a deputy," Clint said. "I'm not even part of your posse. We're just riding together."

"Suits me, however you wanna call it," Tatum said.

"In fact, with that arm you'd be better off going home, too," Clint pointed out.

"I'm not turnin' back," Tatum said.

"You're out of your jurisdiction, aren't you?" Clint asked.

"I still ain't turnin' back," Tatum said. "Dan Magnus was a good deputy, a good man, and they gunned him down like . . ." Tatum stopped, took a deep breath and said again, I ain't turnin' back."

"Okay, fine," Clint said. "But you better get some rest tonight."

"We gotta keep watch."

"I'll split the watch with a couple of your healthier men," Clint said. "In fact, we can give them their choice in the morning, head back or stick it out."

Tatum snorted and said, "They'll all turn back."

"Well," Clint said, "we'll see."

Chapter Twenty-Five

In the morning they gathered the men around and gave them their choice.

"Mr. Adams is joinin' us," the sheriff said, "so you all have a choice. You can return to Rock Springs or come along with us. Those of you who want to go back raise—" He didn't finish his statement when all their hands went up.

"You all want to go back?" Clint asked.

"That's right," Gene said. "We talked about it last night. We're done."

"How the hell—" Tatum started, but Clint cut him off.

"Fine," Clint said. "Break camp and then get going. The sheriff and I need to move immediately."

Clint walked over to Eclipse and began to saddle him. The sheriff came up alongside.

"Which horse is yours?" Clint asked. "I'll saddle him for you."

"I can do it myself."

"Not with that arm," Clint said. "Is that a bullet wound?"

"Yeah, it is."

"Is the bullet still in there?"

"No," Tatum said, "it went right through."

"That's good. When did it happen?"

"A few days ago."

"The robbery was almost two weeks ago, wasn't it?" Clint asked.

"A little more," Tatum said.

"And you caught up to them a few days ago for the first time?"

"They eluded us for a long time," Tatum said. "When we finally caught up to them, it was by accident, and we were all surprised. They reacted faster and better than my men did, and they picked us apart."

"So they must've thought they had lost you."

"I think so."

Clint finished saddling Eclipse and then did Tatum's horse.

"And now? Do they think they're in the clear?"

"Probably," Tatum said. "They might even think I'm dead."

"That's good. When we catch up to them again, they'll be even more surprised."

"And why are you after them?" Tatum asked. "You don't care about the Rock Springs Bank."

Clint finished with Tatum's horse and said, "We can talk about that along the way."

***

"So you don't know if the dead man was your broth-er?" Tatum asked.

"He's not my brother," Clint said. "He could be a step-brother."

"Who you haven't seen for thirty years?"

"Right."

"Then why do you care?"

"I just can't have Quentin going around telling people he killed the Gunsmith's brother."

"Ah," Tatum said, "ego."

"Not at all," Clint said. "It's got nothing to do with my ego."

"Then what?"

"I have to live every day with the thought that some-body might try to kill me."

"Then put your guns down."

"That would never work," Clint said. "I'd be dead even faster."

"Okay, then go on. Why go after Quentin?"

"If people think he killed my brother and got away with it, they'll think I've lost it. If word gets out like that, it would be even worse than me putting my guns down. They'll come for me in droves."

"Okay," Tatum said, "I see. Actually, I don't really care about why you're after him, I'm just glad you are."

"So," Clint said, "how do we track him?"

"He has five men with him," Tatum said. "Luckily, two of them have horses who are leaving recognizable signs."

"So if they split up, we'll be going after them, not knowing if one is him."

"Let's just hope they're still together a while longer," Tatum said.

"Until they're dead sure they've outrun you and your posse," Clint said.

"Yeah."

They rode a while longer before Tatum spoke again.

"If they split up," he said, "we might have to split up, too."

"Are you in shape to ride alone?" Clint asked.

"I suppose that's somethin' we might have to find out," Tatum said. "But first we'll have to find their tracks, again."

"And who was doing your tracking?" Clint asked.

"That'd be me," Tatum said. "Unless you're an expert."

"I've done my share, but I'm no expert," Clint said. "If you've been tracking them, I'll just follow your lead."

"Then let's get to it," Tatum said.

Chapter Twenty-Six

It was later that day when Sheriff Tatum found the sign he was looking for.

"There," he said, pointing.

They both dismounted and knelt down so Tatum could show it to Clint clearly.

"See that nick in the horse's front left?" Tatum said, reaching down to touch it. "And there, that one has a piece of a shoe missing. They'll get that replaced when they can stop for an extended stay somewhere."

"Which hopefully, will be soon," Clint said. "Then we can catch up to them."

"Let's keep goin'," the lawman said. "We still have a couple of hours of light."

As they stood, the man lost his balance and almost tumbled over. Clint reached out and steadied him.

"You need some rest," Clint pointed out.

"I'll get plenty of rest," Tatum said, moving toward his horse, "in two more hours."

They mounted up and continued on.

***

Two-and-a-half hours later, they were camped and sitting around a fire, eating bacon-and-beans.

"I'll stand watch while you get some much needed sleep," Clint said.

"Nonsense," Tatum said. "We don't need you fallin' asleep in your saddle tomorrow."

"Very well," Clint said, "but I need less than you do. I'll wake you when I need to."

"Fine."

Tatum rolled himself up in his bedroll and was asleep in minutes. Clint made another pot of coffee and finished the last of the beans. So far, he knew the sheriff was stubborn, and that he could ride. But he had no idea how effective he would be in a firefight. He was going to have to learn that, and he'd have to learn it right in the action, when they found the bank robbers.

He allowed the lawman a little over five hours sleep before waking him to stand watch. Tatum groaned as he rolled out, but got to his feet and accepted the cup of coffee Clint handed to him.

"There's a fresh pot on the fire," Clint said. "It should be light in two hours. Wake me and we'll get underway."

"Right."

Clint slept for two hours and woke even before Tatum was going to wake him.

As he approached the fire, Tatum held up a cup of coffee for him.

"Feeling okay?" Clint asked.

"A little stiff," Tatum said, "but fine." He flexed the fingers of his left arm, the one in the sling. Clint had noticed earlier that he wore his gun on his right hip, or he never would have ridden with him. "I was thinkin' we'd have some coffee and then get movin'."

"Suits me," Clint said. "After this cup I'll go and saddle the horses."

"How long are you gonna treat me like an invalid?" Tatum asked.

"Until I see that you can toss your saddle up onto your horse's back," Clint said. He finished his coffee and handed the cup back to Tatum. "I'll get to it."

***

They had used the time riding together the day before to get to know each other a little better, and now they did the same. Clint learned some of the other places Tatum had been a lawman—some of them towns unknown to him, but others—like Abilene and Ellsworth—were impressive. You had to be a good lawman to have kept a job in those places for any length of time—not without being fired, but without getting killed.

Clint explained that his days as a lawman had come and gone by the time he was thirty. He just didn't like the limitations the job held, and the political situations it came with. Lastly, he hated dealing with the money men who thought the law was for sale.

"Sometimes," Tatum told him, "you just have to bend a little to get the job done right."

"And that was just the kind of thinking that made me give it up," Clint said. "I'm much better out here on the trail, usually on my own."

"I can't argue with that," Tatum said. "After this mess, Rock Springs just might be the last time I wear a badge."

"Well," Clint said, "we'll just have to see if we can catch Max Quentin and his men, and get that money back to the bank, so you can go out on a high note."

"I'd say I'd drink to that," Sheriff Tatum said, "if I'd thought to bring a bottle of whiskey along."

Chapter Twenty-Seven

Max Quentin was not happy.

That wasn't usually how he felt when he had a big-titted whore in his bed, but even this girl's opulent curves and hot mouth were not improving his mood.

"Whatsamatta, honey?" she asked, from down between his legs. She took his cock in her hand and wriggled it. "You're plenty hard."

"I got other things on my mind," Quentin said, "but that don't mean you gotta stop tryin'."

So she took his cock in her mouth again and continued to suck. Meanwhile, he was thinking of the damn Rock Springs sheriff and his posse. If one of his idiot men hadn't shot a deputy, maybe the lawman wouldn't be so hard on the gang's heels. And shooting them up was no guarantee that they would head back to town. Not when there was a dead lawman involved.

Quentin reached down to hold the girl's head in his hands as it bobbed up and down on him. He and his gang were in the town of Brookline, which consisted of a saloon, a hotel, a whorehouse and a livery stable that was barely standing. They wouldn't be able to stay there much longer, but he had a scout out there, so he'd be able to figure out just how long.

The two groups—the gang and the posse—had ridden into each other completely by chance. He knew that he and his men had shot the posse up pretty good, but one of his men had also been injured. He could have left them behind, but the rest of his men wouldn't have gone for that. On the other hand, he could have just killed him, but again, he'd have to deal with the others. What he needed was time to split the bank proceeds and then have all the men scatter. He'd keep two with him, the two he took on every job, but the others he'd probably never use, or see, again.

Lee Cochran and Buddy Terrell were his regulars. The three of them had been riding together a long time. If he thought the three of them could safely take the other three, he would've killed them all by now and split the money three ways, but that probably wasn't going to happen.

He knew one thing, though. The man who shot the deputy was called Whitey, and he was going to kill him for sure, first chance he got.

At the moment, most of his men were in the saloon, one of them was being treated for his wound by a drunk who claimed he used to be a doctor, and Max Quentin was getting his cock sucked by an over-the-hill blonde whore.

He decided to concentrate on the matter at hand, which was filling this bitch with his seed, which would let off some of the steam that had built up inside of him.

So he closed his eyes and tried to give himself up to the whore's lips and tongue and hands, as she was using every trick she knew to finish him off . . .

***

Cochran and Terrell sat at their table with a bottle of whiskey between them. In the back of the room a man the bartender called "Doc Whiskey" was patching up the gang member who had caught some lead when they clashed with the posse. The other man was standing at the bar. They were all waiting for Skinner, the man Quentin had sent out to check their back trail and see if the posse—what was left of it—was still coming.

And they all knew that Quentin was at the whorehouse, even though he gave orders that nobody else was to go there.

"You think these boys are gonna get all liquored up and try to go over to the whorehouse?" Cochran asked.

"I'll bet," Terrell said, "but hey, that'll give us the excuse we need to shoot 'em."

Cochran laughed and poured them each some more whiskey.

***

"Ahhhhhhhh, shiiiiiiiiiit!" Quentin roared, as his cock seemed to explode.

The whore kept him in her mouth and sucked him until he was completely dry, then released him and smiled up at him.

"That was okay?" she asked.

"Jesus Christ, yes!" he said. "Although it did take a little too long."

"I'm sorry—" she started, but he waved her off.

"Naw, naw, you did fine," he said. "Take the money off the dresser on your way out."

"We're finished?" she asked. There was no inflection or expression to indicate whether or not she was glad they were done.

"We're done, honey," he said, and then added, "for now."

She got off the bed, padded to the dresser naked, took some money, hesitated, then took a little more and hurried for the door, in case he changed his mind.

He knew she wouldn't dare try to take all of his money, and whatever amount she did take, she deserved. He *had* been distracted, which *was* the reason it had taken longer than usual. So let her take what she thought she was owed.

He rolled over in bed, grabbed the makings from the night table and rolled himself a cigarette.

Chapter Twenty-Eight

"What is it?" Sheriff Tatum asked.

"I saw somebody," Clint said.

"Where?"

"Up ahead." Clint pointed.

"I don't see anybody."

"He was on that rise," Clint said.

"What was he doin'?"

"Just watching us," Clint said, "then he turned and rode away."

Tatum stopped looking at the rise, turned his head and looked at Clint.

"A scout?"

"That's what I'm, thinking," Clint said. "So we're not so far behind."

"He's gonna ride back to wherever the gang is and tell Quentin we're comin'."

"Just the two of us," Clint said.

"What would you do if you were him?" Tatum asked.

"I'd wait," Clint said. "I'd just wait for us to catch up. I'd think this is all you have left of your posse, and I'd wait to finish you."

"Well," Tatum said, "Let's hope he does that. I want to see his face when he finds out who I have with me."

"Yes," Clint said, "so do I."

***

Cochran and Terrell looked up at the batwing doors as Bob Skinner came bursting through.

"Where's the boss?" he demanded.

"He's at the whorehouse," Cochran said. "What's goin' on, Bob?"

"I saw them," Skinner said.

"Them?" Terrell said. "The posse?"

"There's only two of them now," Skinner said. "The sheriff's got his arm in a sling, and he's ridin' with one other man."

"Two left," Cochran said. "The boss is gonna like that. Come on, we'll go over to the whorehouse with you."

"I wanna have a beer first," Skinner said.

The three of them went to the bar, tossed down a beer each, then left to go to the whorehouse across the street. The other men—including the injured one—remained in the saloon.

***

117

Max Quentin was getting dressed when there was a knock on his door.

"Yeah, what?"

The door opened and the blonde stuck her head in. She was no longer naked, but wearing a robe, belted tightly at her waist.

"What is it?"

"Three of your men are downstairs," she said. "You wanna come down?"

"No," he said, "send them up."

She nodded and backed out. The next time the door opened Skinner, Cochran and Terrell all walked in.

"What's goin' on?" Quentin asked, from his seated position on the bed.

"I saw what's left of the posse, boss," Skinner said.

"Where?"

"About ten miles back," Skinner said. "They're head-ed this way."

"How many?"

"Two," Skinner said. "Just two."

"Only two left?" Quentin said. "And that stubborn sonofabitch is still comin'?"

"Yes, sir."

"Are you sure it's the sheriff?"

"Yep," Skinner said, "he's still got his arm in a sling."

"Do you know who the man with him is?"

"Nope, never saw 'im before," Skinner said. "He's ridin' a big black horse."

"Yeah, yeah," Quentin said. "Okay, Skinner, get out. Go back to the saloon and wait."

Skinner nodded and left.

"Whataya wanna do, Max?" Cochran asked.

"I ain't sure," Quentin said. "We could wait here for him and finish him."

"That sounds good," Terrell said. "Is there an 'or'?"

"Or we can move on and leave the others here to finish him."

"Don't you wanna finish him yourself?" Cochran asked.

"That don't matter to me," Quentin said. "I just wanna get rid of 'em so we can make the split and move on."

"How much of a split?" Cochran asked.

"I'm still tryin' to decide that," Quentin said. "In this room, we all like three way splits, don't we?"

"We do," Terrell said.

"Well then, if we leave the rest of the men back here to wait for the sheriff, and we move on . . ."

". . . then they should be able to take care of the two man posse . . ." Cochran said.

". . . with a few from our side bein' taken care of, too," Terrell finished.

Quentin smiled.

"It looks like we're all on the same page, then," he said.

Chapter Twenty-Nine

Clint and Sheriff Tatum stopped in front of a signpost.

"Have you ever heard of a town called Brookline?" Clint asked.

"No," Tatum said. "It must be pretty small."

The signpost simply said BROOKLINE, no population, and no mileage.

"It must not be very far," Clint said. "That scout might have come from there."

"That means we can't just ride in, bold as brass," Tatum said.

"Right," Clint said. "We'll have to locate the town, then circle around and come in from the other direction. They won't expect that."

"We'd better get movin', then," Tatum said. "By now that scout has delivered his information."

"That your posse has been busted down to two men," Clint said.

"Luckily," Sheriff Tatum said, "they don't know who the second man is."

***

They came within sight of the town and were surprised.

"There's nothin' there," Tatum said. "Looks like a hotel, a saloon, and another building."

"Mercantile," Clint said, "or maybe a whorehouse."

"I'm gonna say most of the men would be in the saloon," Tatum said.

"I agree."

"That dilapidated building off by itself," Clint said, "could be a livery stable. Why don't we check that out? If it's full of horses, then we'll know they're here."

"Good idea. Plus it's at the far end of the street," Tatum said. "Let's move."

They circled the town and rode in from the far side, stopping at the dilapidated building. They kept it between them and the rest of the town.

They dismounted and Tatum held his forefinger to his lips, just in case there was somebody inside. They moved to the building, stopped to look past the door, which was hanging by one hinge. Inside they saw horses, but no men. They moved inside.

"Let's get a count," Clint said.

"And I wanna check their hooves," Tatum said.

They counted the horses and Tatum lifted their legs to check.

"There are three horses here," Clint said.

"That means about half the gang is in town," Tatum said. "You know what that means."

"Yeah," Clint said, "Quentin lit out and left them here to take care of the two of us."

"We're gonna need at least one alive to tell us where he went," Tatum said, "but it looks like either Quentin or one of the other men is riding that horse with the notched shoe."

"Okay," Clint said, "we might as well go and have a look at the saloon."

"And the whorehouse," Tatum said. "Split up?"

"Yeah," Clint said, "but don't try anything alone. If you find them, come and tell me, and I'll do the same."

"Right."

They left the livery and split up, Clint to the saloon, and Tatum to the whorehouse.

***

As soon as Quentin, Cochran and Terrell left town, Skinner, Whitey and a man named Hanks, decided to take turns at the whorehouse.

Skinner went first, which left Whitey and the injured Hanks in the saloon, nursing beers.

"I don't like this," Hanks said. "You really think they're gonna meet us and give us our cut?"

"They better," Whitey said. "They don't know who they're messin' with if they don't."

"You know," Hanks said, "we wouldn't be here and I wouldn't have a hole in me if you hadn't shot that deputy."

Whitey laughed.

"The sun was shinin' off that badge so bright he was askin' for it," he said.

"Yeah well, that didn't make Quentin happy. Up to now he ain't never killed a lawman."

"And he still ain't," Whitey said. "I have. And when that sheriff gets here, I'm gonna kill me another one."

"Well, I hope they don't get here until I have my turn at the cathouse."

"Don't worry," Whitey said, "after we kill 'em, we'll all have our turn."

"Why are you so blood thirsty all the time?" Hanks asked.

"Hey." Whitey said, "when you're as good with a gun as me, you wanna show it."

Chapter Thirty

Clint looked in the front window of the saloon, saw a bartender behind the bar, and two men standing at it. No one else. He knew he could walk in and handle the both of them with little or no trouble, but he and Tatum had agreed to meet, so he backed off and then headed for the whorehouse.

***

"Well, hello," a blowsy blonde greeted Tatum. "Blonde or brunette, honey?"

"I'm lookin' for a man," the lawman said.

"We don't do that here, honey."

"Do you have any customers right now?"

"Why?"

Tatum showed her his badge, which he had been keeping in his pocket so it wouldn't reflect the sun.

"Yes, Nellie has a man with her," she said.

"One of Max Quentin's gang?"

"They're the only men in town, right now," the girl said.

"So only one is here?"

"Yeah."

"Where?"

"Upstairs."

Tatum turned when Clint came through the front door.

"Blonde or—" the girl started.

"He's with me," Tatum said, cutting her off.

"There are two in the saloon," Clint said.

"And one here," Tatum said. "Upstairs."

"Let's take him first," Clint said, "and keep him alive. Then we can go over to the saloon for the other two."

"You ain't gonna kill 'im here?" the blonde asked, sounding disappointed.

Tatum told her, "Let's see how it goes. Take us to the room he's in."

"Okay," the blonde said, "but don't kill Nellie."

"We'll do our best," Clint promised, and followed her up.

***

There were only two whores in the house, the brunette Nellie and the blonde, Agnes. Skinner had chosen Nellie because she was long and lean, and he liked his women that way.

He was admiring her firm little breasts as they bobbed up and down in front of him, while she bounced on him, when the door to the room slammed open and two men burst in.

The girl screamed and hopped off him, as he tried to roll over and grab his gun, but he was too slow. He was already looking down the barrel of one of their guns.

"Remember me?" the man with a gun said and showed him his badge.

***

Tatum put his gun barrel right in the man's face.

"Come on, honey," Agnes said to Nellie, putting an arm around her, "these fellas have got business."

She rushed the girl out of the room.

Clint moved around to the other side of the bed and tossed the sheet over the naked man.

"Keep that on," he said.

The man ignored the sheet, his eyes fixed on the gun.

"Whataya want?" he demanded.

"What's your name?" Clint asked.

"Skinner."

"Skinner, this is Sheriff Tatum, from Rock Springs. You killed his deputy, remember?"

"Not me," Skinner said, "That was Whitey."

"And where's Whitey now?" Clint asked.

"Over at the saloon," Skinner said. He was finally able to drag his eyes away from Tatum's gun and looked at Clint. "Who're you?"

"He's Clint Adams," Tatum said. "That sound familiar?"

"Aw, Jesus . . ." Skinner moaned.

"Yeah," Tatum said, "exactly. Where's Quentin?"

"He rode out," Skinner said. "He left us here to . . . uh . . ."

"Take care of us?" Clint asked.

"Well, yeah," Skinner said to Clint, "but he didn't know about you."

"But he will," Clint said. "As soon as we catch up to him."

"Now we got an important question, Skinner," Tatum said. "And your life depends on how you answer it."

Skinner swallowed.

"Where is Quentin headed?" Tatum asked.

***

When Clint and Tatum finished with Skinner, they tied him up and left him on the bed. Then they went downstairs.

"Is he dead?" Agnes asked. "Do we gotta clean up blood?"

"He's fine," Tatum said. "We tied him up. Leave 'im that way until we come back."

"Where ya goin'?" Nellie asked.

"Over to the saloon for the other two," Tatum said.

"What if ya don't come back?" Agnes asked, as they went out the door. "What do we do with him?"

"That'll be up to you!" Tatum called back.

Chapter Thirty-One

"How do you want to do this?" Clint asked as they walked.

"Head on," Tatum said.

"You up to it?"

"Hell, yeah," the lawman said.

As they reached the front of the saloon, Tatum took his arm out of the sling and tossed the cloth aside. Then he took out his badge and pinned it on.

"Okay," he said.

They mounted the boardwalk and went through the batwing doors. As they entered, the two men at the bar looked, obviously expecting somebody else.

"Shit," one of them uttered.

"You said a mouthful," Tatum said. "You're both under arrest for bank robbery and murder."

"You can't take us in," one said.

"Not when there's only two of you," added the other.

"We can," Tatum said, "when I'm one, and the other is Clint Adams."

The man who had said "Shit," said it again, and then both men went for their guns.

Clint drew and shot the one on the left. He waited to see how the sheriff would do, and the man did not disappoint. He also drew and shot the man on the right. Both men hit the floor at about the same time.

"Thank you kindly!" the bartender said. "I been waitin' for all these bank robbers to leave, and now they're finally gone."

Clint looked at the man while he replaced the spent round in his gun. The barkeep was in his fifties, built thick enough to take care of most of what came through the batwings. For some reason, Max Quentin was not on that list, so he had just been waiting for them to up and leave.

"How long were they here?" Tatum asked.

"A few days," the barkeep said. "Seemed like they was waitin' for somebody. Maybe you?"

"Maybe."

"Are they all gone?" the bartender asked.

"There's one more at the whorehouse," Clint said. "Alive. We're hoping he'll tell us where the others went."

"You won't need him for that," the man said. "I heard them say they'd meet these men at a town called Church-ill."

"Churchill?" Clint said. He looked at Tatum. "Is that in Wyoming?"

"I never heard of it," Tatum said.

"It's in Colorado," the bartender said, "near Ouray."

Tatum checked the two men to be sure they were dead.

"You fellas want a beer?" the barkeep asked.

"I'll take one," Clint said.

"I find I need a whiskey after killin' a man," Tatum said.

"Comin' up!"

The bartender put their drinks on the bar and said, "On the house, gents. I'll drag these bodies out of my place. You mind if I keep what they got on 'em?"

"It's yours," Tatum said.

While he did that, Clint looked at Tatum and asked, "Are you willing to ride into Colorado for Max Quentin?"

"I'm willin' to ride to hell and back to get that man," Tatum said. "What about you?"

"I've got no problem with jurisdiction," Clint explained.

"I'll deal with that problem when the time comes," Tatum said.

"So what do we do with the other one?" Clint asked. "The one in the whorehouse?"

"We'll question 'im," Tatum, said, "see if what he said jibes with what the bartender told us."

"And then?"

"I don't know," Tatum said. "Takin' him with us might just slow us down. But let's deal with that when the time comes, too."

***

They went back to the whorehouse and untied Skinner.

"What was the shootin'?" Skinner asked.

"Your two friends didn't give us much time to talk," Tatum said.

"They're dead?"

"They are," Clint said.

"Good," Skinner said to Tatum. "That means you killed the man who killed your deputy."

"Which one?" Tatum asked.

"Whitey."

"Which one was he?" Clint asked. "Neither of them had white hair."

"He was the bald one."

"The one I killed," Tatum said, with satisfaction.

"And what was your job?" Clint asked Skinner.

"Lookout," Skinner said, "and scout."

"You never went into the bank?" Tatum asked.

"No."

Tatum looked at Clint, who nodded.

"All right, Skinner," Tatum said, "tell us what we wanna know and you just might walk away from this."

Chapter Thirty-Two

When Clint and Tatum rode into Colorado, the Wyoming lawman put his badge into his pocket for the duration.

"Won't do me any good here, will it?" he said.

"No, it won't."

They started riding, again.

"I've heard of Ouray," Tatum said, "but I don't know where it is."

"I do."

"Have you ever been there?"

"Once."

"So what do you suggest?" Tatum asked. "That we go to Ouray and then find Churchill from there?"

"Exactly."

"Tell me about Ouray?"

"It's in a pocket, surround by mountains," Clint said. "The people are often snowed in."

"This is Fall," Tatum said. "That won't happen now, right?"

"I hope not."

"I hate snow!" Tatum said.

"It's not my favorite thing, either," Clint said. "But you live in Wyoming, so you have to deal with it."

"Yes, I do," Tatum said, "but I hate it, anyway."

"Well, let's just head for Ouray and hope for the best," Clint said.

***

Max Quentin had no intention of meeting up with Skinner and the others in a small town called Churchill. But Churchill was the place he wanted to stop and make the split with Cochran and Terrell.

"If Skinner or any of the others show up," he told them, "we'll kill 'em."

"Suits me," Cochran said.

"Me, too," Terrell said.

"But how long are we gonna stay here?" Cochran asked.

"Yeah," Terrell said, "what if it snows?"

"I'm meetin' with a man to plan our next job," Quentin said, "and he wants that meet to be here, in Churchill."

"So give us our split and we'll go," Cochran suggested. "You can have your meet."

"If the meet goes well," Quentin said, "we'll be pullin' the job in the next few days. I don't wanna hafta go lookin' for you."

"So you want us to stay around," Terrell said.

"Right," Quentin said. "There are two saloons in town. Pick one."

"A whorehouse?" Cochran asked.

"There is one," Quentin said, "but stay away from it."

"Fine," Terrell said.

"And if Skinner or the others show up," Quentin said, "take care of them."

"What about that sheriff?" Cochran asked.

"If he shows up, take care of him, too."

"Okay," Cochran said.

"And you two," Quentin said, "stay together, just in case that does happen."

"Beer?" Cochran asked Terrell.

"I thought you'd never ask."

Together, they left Max Quentin's room, which was down the hall from the one they were sharing in the Churchill Hotel.

Quentin moved to the window and looked down at Front Street—the only street in Churchill that had a name. He watched as Cochran and Terrell left the hotel and went across the street to the Lexington Saloon.

There was nobody else on the street. In the distance, the tops of the San Juan Mountains were covered with snow. He hoped the snow wouldn't move on down to the town. He didn't need to get snowed in.

He toyed with the idea of leaving Churchill, not meeting with a man named Pritchard, not splitting with Cochran and Terrell, and keeping the proceeds of the Rock Springs bank job for himself. But he had been riding with Cochran and Terrell for a long time, so in the end he decided to stay and wait for Pritchard. He hoped that the job the man was proposing was worth the wait.

***

Clint and Sheriff Tatum rode through the San Juan Mountains to Ouray without encountering the snow that was covering the mountain tops. Snowstorms at this time of the year were rare, and light. Clint decided not to compound the problem by worrying about it.

As they rode into Ouray Clint noticed that Tatum's horse was laboring. He'd been noticing the horse's problems for a few miles. The animal simply could not keep up with Eclipse.

"You need another horse," he said, "and mine needs some rest."

Tatum stroked his animal's neck. "You're right. I don't wanna ride this one into the ground. Let's see if somebody here has a horse for sale."

"It's early," Clint said. "Let's try to do it today so we can ride out tomorrow for Churchill."

"Agreed."

Chapter Thirty-Three

They found a man in town who had two horses for sale in his corral, a five-year-old mustang, and a seven-year-old spotted mare.

"I'll take the mare," Tatum said.

"Why not the mustang?" the man asked.

"What am I gonna do with a mustang?" the lawman asked. "I need a solid, reliable horse. The mare will do."

The man looked at Clint, who just shrugged, so the man shrugged, too, adding a head shake, and took the mustang back to the corral.

"I know," Tatum said, as he put his saddle on the mare, "don't say it."

"Hey," Clint said, "as long as you're not cutting and roping and . . . working a herd, you sure don't need the mustang."

"Just what I was thinkin'." Sheriff Tatum had insisted on saddling his own mount, so Clint simply stood aside and watched him struggle, but get it done. He gave the cinch one last yank and then stepped back. "Looks okay."

"Good," Clint said. "So you don't need a new saddle."

The man came back and they arranged to have their horses—Eclipse and the new mare—boarded with him overnight.

"One night?" he asked.

"Just one night," Clint said.

"Okay."

"How many hotels are in town?" Tatum asked.

"Just The Palace," the man said. "Down the street."

"Yeah, we passed it on the way in," Clint said.

They collected their rifles and bedrolls and told the man to have the horses ready at first light. Then they headed to the hotel on foot.

**

They got a room each at The Palace Hotel, then ate in the Palace dining room.

"This town looks a little bigger than Brookline, and that was just three buildings," Tatum said.

"Four, if you count the livery stable."

"That probably fell down after we left," Tatum said. He fed some stew into his mouth. "The food's good here. My room's okay, too. How's yours?"

"Good."

"And the steak?"

"Also good."

"We passed a few private homes on the way in," Tatum said. "This could be a little paradise."

"You want to stay here?" Clint asked. "Retire? Send your badge back to Rock Springs?"

"No," Tatum said. "But hey, maybe when I am ready to retire, this wouldn't be such a bad place. How far are we from Denver?"

"Oh, a pretty good ways," Clint said. "Probably three hundred miles."

"I wonder how far we are from Churchill?" Tatum said.

"A lot closer than three hundred miles," Clint said. "We should be there tomorrow."

"That's good," Tatum said. "Maybe we can bring all this to an end."

"One way or another," Clint said.

"What's that mean?"

"I mean whether Max Quentin is there or not. You're probably going to have to head home. You got half the bank robbers, including the man who killed your deputy."

"But I didn't recover any money," Tatum said.

"The money was never your objective," Clint pointed out.

"Still," Tatum said, "I'm the sheriff and I've been away a long time. I gotta come back with somethin'."

"You could've gone back with Skinner."

"And no money," Tatum said. "My first reason for bein' out here may not have been the money, but I've been gone too long to return empty handed.

"You're probably right about that, Sheriff," Clint said. "But let's see what we can do about it when we get to Churchill."

"I'm just thinkin', Clint," Tatum went on, "what if Quentin never had any intention of meetin' Skinner and the others there?"

"There's no point in worrying about that now," Clint commented. "Let's just wait and see what we find when we get there."

Tatum nodded.

"You're probably right," the lawman said.

"I think I am," Clint said, "so let's just finish eating, have a drink, and then get some rest."

"Agreed," Tatum said.

Chapter Thirty-Four

The snow stayed on the mountain tops and did not come down to town, so when Clint and Tatum rose the next morning, it was cold and sunny. There was nothing to keep them from leaving Ouray.

The road to Churchill became hazardous, at times, alternately narrow and steep, sometimes making it necessary to dismount and walk the horses.

"If they run, this would make for a helluva chase," Tatum commented.

"And it's not much better on the other side, as I remember," Clint said.

Eventually, they got to the point where they were once again able to ride.

"How do you want to play this, Sheriff?" Clint asked. He had been thinking about this ever since the sheriff had mentioned that he needed to bring something back to Rock Springs—preferably the money. "Do you want to try to take them alive?"

"Until we have the money, we need at least one of them alive," he said. "If they made the split and went their separate ways, though, we're probably gonna be out of luck."

Clint was going to leave that call to the lawman because he didn't want the money, he just wanted Max Quentin.

***

Max Quentin looked up from his beer and saw the man enter the small saloon. It had been a few years, but he recognized Aaron Pritchard right away. He didn't know the three men with him, but assumed they were gang members.

Pritchard saw Quentin, spoke to his men, and as he approached the table, they went to the bar.

"Max," Pritchard said.

"Aaron." Quentin got to his feet to shake hands, and then they sat. One of Pritchard's men brought two fresh beers over to the table and returned to the bar. All three of them looked to be in their late twenties, or early thirties. Pritchard himself was about Quentin's age, mid-forties.

"That's a young bunch," he commented to Pritchard.

"That's because the older ones are dead," Pritchard said. He was a well-spoken man, educated in the East. "That's why you have to cultivate the young ones."

"I guess you're right," Quentin said.

Pritchard sat back in his chair.

"I hear you're making a name for yourself, these days," he said. "'The Man Who Killed the Gunsmith's brother?'"

"Is that gettin' around, already," Quentin asked, not displeased with the comment.

"You should know," Pritchard said. "You're the one who's been spreading the word."

"Why did you pick such an out-of-the-way place for us to meet, Aaron?" Quentin asked.

"So we wouldn't be seen together," Pritchard said. "I don't want anyone to see this coming."

"The job?"

"Us working together," Pritchard said. "We've each made our mark working apart. No point in letting people know we're going to join forces."

"Are we?"

"I hope so," Pritchard said.

"Well," Quentin said, "I guess that's gonna be up to me, once I hear what the job is."

"Can we do that over something to eat?" Pritchard asked. "I'm starving."

"We've only been here a couple of days," Quentin said. "I don't know where we can get a good meal. Our hotel dining room is probably only good for breakfast. And this place only does sandwiches."

"I've been here before," Pritchard said. "It's why I chose it." He stood up. "I know a good place to eat."

Quentin stood up.

"Then I'll follow you," he said.

***

At one point, Clint and Sheriff Tatum found themselves looking down at the town of Churchill. It was a collection of buildings with a couple of streets crisscrossing, but there was no obvious path to it.

"What are we supposed to do?" Tatum said. "Jump."

"There's got to be a way down," Clint said, looking around. "We'll probably have to walk the horses, again."

"I hope we find some food when we get there," Tatum said.

"It's a town, Sheriff," Clint said. "I'm sure there'll be places to eat."

"Lately," Tatum said, "the word 'town' is bein' used real loosely."

Clint knew what he meant, considering some of the places they'd been, like Brookline and Ouray.

"Hopefully," Clint said, "things will look better once we actually get down there.

Chapter Thirty-Five

They entered through a doorway in the back of the building.

"I never woulda found this place," Quentin said. He looked around at the other four tables, which were empty at the moment.

"You have to know it's here," Pritchard said.

"How often do you come here?" Quentin asked.

"I'll tell you something nobody knows," Pritchard said. "Just to show you that I trust you."

"Go ahead."

"I live here."

"In this hole?"

"It's not a hole," Pritchard said. "It's peaceful and quiet, and that's what I like when I'm planning my jobs."

"Like the one I'm about to hear?"

"Yes," Pritchard said. "Like that one . . ."

A young waiter came over.

"Nice to see ya, Mr. Pritchard," the young man said. "Beef stew today?"

"Yes, James, as usual." Pritchard looked at Quentin. "Best stew you'll ever have."

"Then I guess I'll have the beef stew," Quentin said to the waiter.

"Good choice, gents," the waiter said with a smile, and hurried away.

"Now," Pritchard said, "the job . . ."

***

Clint and Tatum finally found a path they were able to walk their horses down.

"If I'd known about this I woulda bought that sure-footed little mustang," Tatum complained.

"These two are doing just fine," Clint said. "The mare was a good choice."

When they made it down to flat ground, they were able to mount up.

"We're further from the town than I thought, when we were looking down at it," the lawman said.

"Yeah, it's almost like a . . . mirage . . . no, an illusion . . . from up there."

"So how much longer?" Tatum asked,

"Now that we're on flat ground," Clint answered, "maybe a couple of hours."

"There better be a place to eat."

***

"Denver?" Quentin asked.

"It would be the biggest score either one of us have ever had," Pritchard said.

"Yeah, but Denver?" Quentin said. "They've got a big police department, marshals, a sheriff—"

"And banks with a lot of money," Pritchard said. "Enough for all of us, you, me, and our men. You do have men with you, don't you?"

"A couple."

"Cochran and Terrell, right? You're still riding with them?"

"I am."

"Good," Pritchard said, "we're going to need men with experience—not like these young pups I have riding with me, now."

"You're not fillin' me with a lot of confidence, Aaron," Quentin said.

"This is why I want you, Max," Pritchard said. "You have the brains, the experience, and the men."

"And what do you have?" Quentin asked.

As the waiter appeared at that moment with two steaming bowls Pritchard smiled and said, "I have the stew."

***

When the town finally appeared up ahead of them Tatum asked, "Is that it, for real, this time?"

"That's it."

"Does Churchill have a lawman?" Tatum asked.

"I know about the town's existence because I've been to Ouray," Clint said. "But I don't know that."

"Then I guess we'll find out after we get there," Tatum said.

"You might end up being the only badge-toter there," Clint said.

"A badge with no jurisdiction in Colorado," Tatum reminded him.

"Yeah, but still a badge," Clint said. "It might come in handy."

Tatum touched his pocket where his tin star was residing at the moment and said, "Well, if we need it, I've got it right here."

Chapter Thirty-Six

"When?" Quentin asked Pritchard.

"As soon as we plan it, and outfit ourselves," Pritchard said.

"We're gonna plan it?"

"You *are* usually the brains behind your jobs, right?" Pritchard said.

"Yeah, so?"

"So I didn't assume you were going to allow me to plan it and just follow."

"Yeah, okay," Quentin said. "But I usually take a look at a bank before I hit it."

"Denver's only three hundred miles away from here," Pritchard said.

"Only?" Quentin repeated. "Are you tryin' to convince me *not* to go?"

"I thought since I already looked the bank over—" Pritchard started, with a shrug.

"You have a plan in mind already, don't you?" Quentin asked.

"Sort of . . . but subject to your approval, of course."

"Without seein' the bank for myself," Quentin added.

"Well, like I said," Pritchard replied, "I've already looked it over."

Quentin looked down at his empty stew bowl.

"Is there a better place in this town to get a drink than that saloon we were in?"

"Yes, there is," Pritchard said. "My house."

***

Clint and Tatum finally rode into the town of Church-ill.

"Is this a ghost town?" Tatum asked, searching the empty street.

"I don't think so."

"No," Tatum said, looking down, "some of these tracks are fresh, but . . . where is everybody?"

They reined in their horses in front of a small saloon.

"Maybe in there," Clint suggested.

They dismounted. Clint dropped Eclipse's reins to the ground, waited for Tatum to tie his mare to the hitching rail, and then entered.

"Welcome," the bartender said, with a smile.

"Where is everyone?" Tatum asked, looking around the interior. There were perhaps half-a-dozen handmade tables and chairs.

"Everybody's tendin' to their own business," the bartender said. "What can I do for you gents? Are you lost?"

"What makes you think we're lost?" Clint asked, as he and Tatum approached the bar.

"Well," the middle-aged bartender said, "that's usually the only way folks come wanderin' into Churchill, if they're lost."

"We're not lost," Tatum said, "and we're thirsty. Two beers."

"Comin' up."

As he set the mugs down in front of them Clint asked, "Is there another saloon in town?"

"Whatsamatta with this one?" the man asked.

"It's kind of quiet."

"Yeah, there's another one," the bartender said.

"Where?" Clint asked.

"Spittin' distance," the man said, "but then everythin' is spittin' distance around here."

"Is it like this one?" Tatum asked. "Small and quiet?"

"It's bigger," the bartender said, "and it gets noisier at night."

"Any other strangers in town?" Tatum asked.

"Uh-oh," the bartender said.

"What?" Tatum asked.

"You're law."

"Not around here I ain't."

"Who you lookin' for?" the bartender asked.

"We're looking for a man named Max Quentin," Clint said. "Do you know him?"

"I heard of him," the bartender said, "but not around here. Of course, I coulda served him a beer and never known 'im."

"True," Tatum said. "He's not gonna walk in and announce himself."

"Have any other strangers wandered in here, lost?" Clint asked. "You didn't answer that question."

"If they did ride in, they didn't come in here, but that ain't no surprise."

Tatum looked at Clint.

"We better check the other saloon."

Clint looked at the bartender.

"Is there a hotel in town?"

"Sure," the man said, "but every room's gonna be covered in dust."

"Should be cheap, then," Clint said.

The bartender laughed as they went out the door and called to them, "You'd think, huh?"

Chapter Thirty-Seven

Aaron Pritchard's house was above Churchill, so he could look down on it whenever he wanted to.

"How'd you get this house?" Quentin asked, as they walked to the door.

"Easy," Pritchard said, "nobody else wanted it."

"I can see why," Quentin said. "That was a long walk up here."

"Yeah, but look at the view," Pritchard said.

Quentin turned and found himself looking at the haphazardly placed buildings that made up Churchill.

"Why wouldja wanna look down on that?" he asked.

"That's easy," Pritchard said. "I own it."

"Own what?" Quentin asked.

"The whole town," Pritchard said. "I own Churchill."

"What?"

Pritchard walked to the front door, unlocked it and went in, leaving it open behind him.

"Hey, wait!" Max Quentin said, following him. "What the hell?"

***

"This town makes me nervous," Sheriff Tatum said.

"I'll tell you what makes me nervous," Clint said, looking up. "All those houses above us."

"Yeah," Tatum said. "Anybody could be up there with a rifle."

"I wonder if most of the people in town live up there," Clint said, "and not down here."

"The whole place is odd."

They found the larger saloon. The smaller one had no name, but this one had a board over the door with SULLY'S SALOON written on it in charcoal.

As they entered, they saw the difference right away. There were more tables and chairs, better quality, a longer bar, and there were actually customers standing at it. At one of the tables, two men in their late thirties sat drinking beer, just watching.

The men wore trail clothes and guns on their hips. They turned as Clint and Tatum entered. The bartender, who had been leaning with his elbows on the bar, straightened and watched as they approached. Clint didn't recognize any of the men, or the bartender. They all looked to be in their late twenties, the bartender his late fifties.

"Help you gents?" the barkeep asked.

"Two beers," Tatum said.

"Looks like we're not the only ones who got lost up here," Clint said, nodding at the three men.

They laughed and one said, "Oh, we ain't lost. We know exactly where we're at, don't we, boys?"

The other two nodded.

"Well, that's good for you, then," Clint said.

Instinctively, he knew not to mention Max Quentin's name to these men.

The bartender put their drinks on the bar.

"So what're ya lookin' for, if yer lost?" the bartender asked.

"A town called Ouray," Tatum said.

Clint was glad to see that the lawman had the same instincts. Some or all of the five men might've been riding with Quentin.

"You gotta go west a few miles," the bartender said. "Ain't gonna be easy goin', though, so it'll take a while."

"Well," Clint said, "is there a hotel in town?"

"I guess you could call it that," the bartender said. "Don't usually have any guests, though. Not sure they even know how to treat some."

"I guess we'll have to chance it," Clint said. "How much for the beers?"

"On the house," the bartender said, "Seein' as how yer only here because yer lost."

They drained their beers and said, "Thanks."

All five men watched them leave the saloon.

"Whataya think?" Tatum asked.

"I was going to ask you that," Clint said. "Do you think any of those men could've been with Max Quentin in Rock Springs?"

"Not the three at the bar," Tatum said, "but maybe the other two. One of the tellers described a couple of the men bein' in their thirties."

"And we already took care of the younger ones, right?" Clint said.

"Right."

"So if those two are with Quentin, where is he?" Clint asked.

"Maybe in the hotel," Tatum said, "or maybe up in one of those houses."

"Let's start with the hotel," Clint said. "Where did that bartender say it was?"

Chapter Thirty-Eight

The first bartender had been right. As they approached the front desk, they could see that it—and the lobby—were covered with dust.

There was nobody manning the front desk. They didn't know if that was normal or not. Behind the desk all the room keys were hanging on the wall.

"They're all there," Clint said.

"So either they have no guests, or the guests dropped their keys off at the desk when they went out."

"Anybody here?" Clint yelled. "Hello?" He banged his hand on the desk. There was no bell.

Suddenly, a man came out from the back, his hair in disarray. He was about sixty.

"Help ya?"

"We need two rooms," Clint said.

"Yer kiddin'."

"He's not," Tatum said.

The man cackled and waved his arms at the keys.

"Pick any two."

"Something away from the front of the building," Clint said.

"I'm gonna give ya one and two," the man said, snatching the keys.

"Anybody else in the hotel?"

"You gotta be kiddin'."

"How much?" Tatum asked.

"Who the hell knows?" the man asked. "Pay me what ya want when ya leave." He waved and went back to his nap in the back room.

As they walked up the stairs, Clint said to the lawman, "Where do you suppose those five men from the saloon are sleeping tonight?"

"Who knows?" Tatum said. "But I sure hope the locks on these doors work."

***

Max Quentin stared down at the hand drawn diagram on the table.

"You've got this whole thing mapped out," he said, almost accusingly.

"I need the right men to pull it, Max," Pritchard said, unapologetically. "That's not me and mine, it's you and your boys."

Quentin studied the diagram a little longer, then looked at Pritchard.

"So, I guess I'll be sleepin' up here while we're in town?" he asked.

"My guest."

"And where do my men sleep? The hotel?"

Pritchard snorted.

"That dust trap? No, they'll sleep where my men are sleeping, in a house across the way."

"And you own these houses, too?"

"Of course."

"All of 'em?" Quentin asked.

"Just the ones worth owning."

"Then why do you need to pull this job if you own a town?" Quentin asked.

"It's jobs like this that allow me to buy towns, Max," Pritchard said. "After this one, you could own a town, if you want to."

"That's not somethin' I've ever wanted," Quentin said, "but I can still see the appeal of the job."

At that point, there was a knock at the door.

"Hang on."

Pritchard went to the door. Quentin could hear the drone of a conversation taking place, and then he was back with one of his men.

"Tell him what you just told me, Lonny," Pritchard told his man.

Lonny turned to face Quentin.

"Two strangers rode into town," he said.

"And?" Quentin asked.

"They stopped in both saloons. The bartender in the No Name said they asked about you."

"You got a posse on your tail, Max?" Pritchard asked.

"I did," Quentin said. "These two are probably the last ones left."

"You should've told me that," Pritchard said. "This doesn't make me very happy."

"Don't worry about it," Quentin said. "They started with a dozen, and there's two left. Me and my boys will take care of them."

"You'd better," Pritchard said. "I don't like having lawmen in my town."

"Just tell your men to stay out of it," Quentin said. "We can handle it."

"Pass the word," Pritchard told his man. "I don't want you or the others even on the street."

"Right, boss."

The man left and Pritchard turned, but before he could speak, Quentin said, "We'll take care of them, Aaron, and then we're goin' to Denver."

Chapter Thirty-Nine

Clint and Tatum took two rooms, but decided to both stay in one, so they could each get some sleep while the other watched his back.

There was a small stable behind the hotel, where they boarded their horses, then took their rifles and bedrolls into the hotel with them.

"I wish we had a room overlookin' the front," Tatum said.

"That would make it too easy for somebody to take a shot at us through the window," Clint said.

"I guess you're right," Tatum said.

"Why don't you get some sleep first," Clint suggested, "and I'll stand watch."

"I ain't gonna argue with you," the lawman said. "Wake me whenever you like."

Tatum went to the bed, fell on it fully dressed, and was asleep in moments.

Clint kept his gun on, as well as his boots, sat in the one wooden chair in the room, facing the door. If someone came through the door it wouldn't matter who it was, he'd draw and fire.

Tatum started to snore, which was good. It would help keep Clint awake.

***

Max Quentin walked into Sully's Saloon, looked around, then walked to the table where his men were seated.

"What's goin' on?" Cochran asked, as he sat.

"There's two strangers in town," Quentin said. "You see 'em?"

"Yeah, they was in here," Terrell said. "Why?"

"They ask about me?"

"No," Cochran said.

"Well, they did in the other saloon," Quentin said.

"So you think it's the two who're left from the posse?" Terrell asked.

"It's gotta be," Quentin said. "Nobody else is gonna be lookin' for me."

"Whataya wanna do?" Cochran asked.

"We got a big job ahead of us," Quentin said, "but before we can get to it, we gotta take care of what's left of that posse."

"Now?" Terrell asked.

"Do we know where they are?" Quentin asked.

"Well," Cochran said, "maybe the hotel."

"We can't do nothin' until we know exactly where they are," Quentin said. "So we'll take them tomorrow."

Cochran looked over at the men at the bar, who were drinking with their backs to the room.

"What about them?"

"No," Quentin said, "this is gonna be just us. After all, the posse's after us."

"Two men left," Cochran said. "This shouldn't be hard."

"Do we know if one of them is that sheriff from Rock Springs?" Quentin asked.

"No, we don't," Terrell said.

"Okay," Quentin said, "you go to that other saloon and find out what you can. Cochran, find out where those two posse men are right now."

"Okay," Cochran said, standing.

As the two men left, Quentin stood up and walked to the bar.

"Beer," he said to the bartender. He stood apart from Pritchard's three men.

"There ya go," the barman said, setting a cold one down.

From an end of the bar one of the younger men said, "Your boys need any help, Quentin?"

"They're just fine, thanks," Quentin said. "I think your boss might be lookin' for you fellas, though."

He saw Lonny, who brought Pritchard the message about the two posse members, frown.

"Yeah, he asked me to send you on up," Quentin continued.

The other two looked at Lonny, and then all three men shrugged and left the saloon.

"Young pups," the bartender said.

"They'll learn," Quentin said, "but probably the hard way."

"Is there any other way?" the bartender asked.

"What about you?" Quentin asked.

"Whataya mean?"

"The two men who came in," Quentin said. "Did you know them?"

"Never saw them before."

"And they didn't say who they were or why they're here?" Quentin asked.

"Said they was lost, is all," the bartender replied.

"And did you send them to the hotel?"

"They asked about it, so yeah," the bartender said, "but I told them it didn't get much use, these days."

If they were from the posse, they'd probably prefer the hotel to be empty, Quentin reasoned to himself.

He drank half his beer, set it down, said, "Thanks," and left.

Chapter Forty

There were a couple of chairs out in front of Sully's Saloon. Max Quentin sat in one and prepared to wait. It didn't take long. As it started to get dark, Cochran came back from the first saloon. He sat in the other chair.

"The bartender said one of them was the law," he said.

"That sheriff," Quentin said.

"The man told the bartender he wasn't the law around here."

"Right. And the other man?"

"Didn't say who he was."

"No name?"

"Nothin'."

Both men looked up as Terrell came back.

"So?"

"They're in the hotel," Terrell said. "They each took a room."

"Did they sign the register?"

"Ain't no register."

"That figures," Quentin said. "Do you know what rooms they're in?"

"One and two."

"Okay," Quentin said, "maybe we can do this to-night."

***

Lonny and the other two looked at their boss, Pritchard, who was staring at them from his doorway, clad in only a bathrobe.

"Your friend, Quentin, said you wanted us up here," Lonny said.

"Yeah, well, that's because he didn't want you down there," Pritchard said.

"So what do we do?" Lonny asked.

"Stay out of the way," Pritchard said. "Turn in for the night."

"This early?"

"You've got nothing else to do."

"We need some whores up here," Lonny said. "Then we'd have somethin' to do."

"I'll take that under advisement," Pritchard promised. "Stay out of town until morning. Understand?"

"Yes, sir."

Pritchard closed his door.

"What's he care?" one of the other men said. "He's got his own whore in there."

"She's his woman," Lonny said, as they went back down the street. "not his whore."

"Same thing."

"Better not let him hear you say that," Lonny warned. "Come on. We're turnin' in."

They went back down the walk.

***

Pritchard returned to his bedroom, where his woman, Hannah Gill, waited in his bed.

"What did they want?" she asked.

"Whores," he said, removing his robe. He was naked underneath. As he approached the bed, she reached out and stroked his semi-hard cock.

Hannah lived in Denver, but had decided to accompany him on this trip back to Churchill. She wanted to see this town he had told her he owned.

She was in her thirties, firmly built, with red hair and a not pretty-but-interesting face. She had a few freckles around her nose, more on her neck and shoulders, and even more the further down you went.

She closed her hand over him and tugged.

"Are we gonna be interrupted anymore?" she asked.

"We better not be," he said, getting on the bed with her.

"And when are we heading back to Denver?"

"Oh, in a day or two," he said. "Why?" He touched her firm breast, her nipple, with the tip of his finger. "Don't you like my little town?"

"Honestly?" she asked.

"I asked, didn't I?"

"I like my town better," she said.

"Well," he said, "Denver is different."

"Is it?" she asked. "This place is a ghost town."

"I like it that way," he said.

"Well," she said, "I need a little more activity."

He slid his hand down over her belly and between her legs, where he probed, finding her wet.

"I can give you some more activity," he said.

She bit her lip as he moved his finger.

He kissed her, and then began to kiss her neck, still moving his finger.

"Are you going to stay in Denver with me, Aaron?" she whispered.

"Honey," he said, with his lips still on her skin, "I'm going to buy you Denver."

Chapter Forty-One

Clint stirred as soon as Tatum touched his arm.

"Somebody's in the hall," the lawman whispered.

Clint rolled out of bed, still wearing his gun. He motioned to Tatum to get down behind the bed. Then he took up a position so that he'd be behind the door when it opened.

They both listened intently to the hallway floor creaking under somebody's feet. There was no light coming beneath the door. From outside the room, if they bothered to look, they would have seen the same thing. Everybody was in the dark, but there was a window in the room, and some moonlight. Clint and Tatum had a slight advantage.

It sounded like whoever was in the hall had stopped in front of the door. Clint waited to see if the door would open, but in the end whoever it was went back down the hall, and then the floor stopped creaking.

"What was that about?" Tatum whispered.

"Scouting mission, I bet," Clint said. "Stay there."

Clint stepped to the other side of the door, then grabbed the door knob and swung it open. The hallway was empty. Clint closed the door.

"They decided against it, probably because there's no light," he said. "That means they'll come for us in the daylight tomorrow."

"Let 'em come," Tatum said. "We'll be ready."

***

Max Quentin and Cochran were waiting just outside the hotel for Terrell when he came back down.

"Well?" Quentin asked.

"I did what you told me to do," Terrell said. "Walked around in the hall, made sure they heard me."

"And? Did a light go on in the room?"

"No."

"So they were waitin' in the dark," Quentin said. "They were ready for us, even if you hadn't stomped around in the hall."

"Looks like it," Terrell said.

"So whatta we do?" Cochran asked.

"We wait for tomorrow," Quentin said. "We take 'em in the daylight."

"They'll really be ready, then," Terrell said.

"Yeah, well, so will we," Quentin said. "Come on."

***

Clint turned the lamp up on the wall by the door.

"They're not comin' back," Tatum said. "Not to-night."

"The light's for us, not them," Clint said.

"Ain't you goin' back to sleep?"

"I'm not tired," Clint said. "You can lie down again, if you want."

"Naw, not me," Tatum said.

"How's your arm?"

"I'm fine, Clint. I'll be ready for tomorrow."

"Yeah, well," Clint said, thoughtfully, "the problem is, so will they."

"There's three of 'em, and two of us," Tatum said. "I think we can handle 'em."

"Well, after that little scouting mission just now, I'm thinking there may be more than three."

"You think Quentin recruited some other men?" Tatum asked. "Here?"

"We saw three men in the saloon," Clint said. "Could be he's already done it."

"So five, then," Tatum said.

Clint nodded.

"That changes the odds, just a little," he said.

"Are you worried?"

Clint didn't answer.

"I understand you don't know how I'll react when the shooting starts, whether or not I can watch your back. But I've worn a badge a long time, Clint, and I've been through this before."

"I figured."

"And you don't have to worry about this," Tatum continued, lifting his injured left arm. "It won't keep me from being effective."

"I'm not worried," Clint said. "I'm concerned about my goal, in all this."

"Which is?"

"To make sure that rumor about Quentin killing the Gunsmith's brother doesn't spread," Clint said. "I want people to know it didn't happen. I can't have them thinking it did, and I did nothing about it."

"So takin' care of him in this tiny little mountain town might not do that," Tatum said. "No witnesses."

"Right."

"Well then," Tatum said, "I'll just have to come out of this alive, so I can spread the word."

"That *would* be helpful," Clint admitted.

Chapter Forty-Two

By the time the sun came up Tatum had drifted off again, while Clint sat in the chair and watched the door. As the sun rose, he woke the lawman.

"Breakfast," he said.

"I hope we have time to eat it before we have to kill somebody," Sheriff Tatum said, rolling out of bed. As Clint had done the night before, the lawman had slept with his gun still strapped on.

They went downstairs, where their passing through the hotel lobby stirred the dust on everything, including the empty front desk.

"We could leave some money," Tatum said.

"Let's settle up later," Clint said, "before we leave town."

Tatum felt that was assuming they were alive to leave town, but didn't offer that thought aloud.

They stepped outside and stopped.

"I wonder where you go to get something to eat in this town?" Tatum said.

"Only one way to find out."

They started walking, very aware of the houses that loomed above the town, and the vantage point they offered anyone with a rifle and a notion of ambush.

***

Max Quentin was having breakfast in the café Aaron Pritchard had taken him to the day before. He assumed that in looking for a place to eat, the sheriff and his posse members would find the place. He had his men positioned outside, to wait.

He wanted to have a talk with the sheriff before they killed him.

***

"There," Clint said, pointing. "That looks like a place to eat."

"An out-of-the-way place," Tatum said, "off the main street."

"What's the difference?" Clint asked. "There's nobody on either street."

Tatum put his hand out to stop Clint before they approached it.

"If it's the only place in town to eat, the gang might be in there," Tatum said.

"We'll just be ready for that," Clint said.

Tatum nodded, and they approached the door. This time Clint put his hand out to stop Tatum.

"What is it?" Tatum asked.

"We're being watched," Clint said.

"We knew that."

"They'll hit us when we come out," Clint said.

"We knew that, too," Tatum said. "At least it'll happen on a full stomach."

Clint dropped his hand from the sheriff's arm, and they entered.

***

"We shoulda took 'em now," Cochran said.

"Quentin said not to," Terrell reminded him. "He said to wait until they come out."

"I know that," Cochran said, "but we shoulda made up our own minds."

"Quentin's the boss," Terrell said. "He always has been."

"Yeah," Cochran said, "I know."

"So now we just wait," Terrell said, folding his arms.

***

Pritchard had arranged for the café to be empty when Quentin went in, so he was the only diner as Clint and Tatum entered the small place.

"Ah, I see," Clint said.

"What?" Tatum asked.

"That's got to be our man," Clint said. "Max Quentin, himself."

"You think so?"

"Let's ask," Clint suggested.

They walked to the table.

"Max Quentin?" Tatum asked.

"You're the sheriff," Quentin said.

"Tatum," the lawman said, "Sheriff Tatum, from Rock Springs. I've tracked you all the way here."

"Where you have no jurisdiction," Quentin pointed out.

"That may be," Clint said, "but I don't need jurisdiction."

"Because you're a posse member, but not a lawman?" Quentin asked.

"No," Clint said, "because my name is Clint Adams."

Chapter Forty-Three

"Now I get it," Max Quentin said. "Why don't you gents sit down and have some breakfast?"

They stared at him.

"No, no, I mean it," Quentin said. "On me. Look, my friend owns the town and he doesn't allow any shootin' in here. I just ordered."

Clint and Tatum exchanged a glance, and then Clint nodded. They sat. He claimed the chair that would give him a good view of the door.

"Hey Jasper!" Quentin yelled. "Make that three?" He looked at Clint and Tatum, "Steak-and-eggs okay?"

"Fine," Clint said.

"Well, Sheriff," Quentin said, "where's the rest of your posse, and how'd you join up with the Gunsmith?"

"You killed or drove off my posse," Tatum said. "I got lucky and met up with Mr. Adams. He told me why he's after you, so we joined forces."

"Ah," Quentin said, turning his head to look at Clint, "the brother thing, right?"

"Not my brother," Clint said.

"What?"

"The man you killed wasn't my brother," Clint clarified.

"But he was tellin' everybody he was," Quentin complained.

"He was confused."

"Well, I'll be damned," Quentin said, "and here I thought I had me a new reputation."

"The man who killed the Gunsmith's brother?" Clint said. "That's a reputation worth having?"

"You're probably right," Quentin said. "Why worry about that when I got somethin' better right in front of me."

"The man who killed the Gunsmith?" Clint asked.

"Why not?"

Clint leaned forward and said, "Because it's not going to happen."

The waiter came out with three plates and Clint sat back. Despite the company, the food smelled good and his stomach started to growl.

"Why don't we talk after we eat?" Quentin said. "I don't know about you two, but I'm hungry."

They started eating . . .

***

Clint kept his eyes on the door the entire time, not trusting Quentin's comment about his friend's rule.

"You've gotta relax, Adams," Quentin said, at one point. "Nothin's gonna happen in here."

"You'll excuse me if I don't take your word for that, Quentin."

"Well, then," Quentin said, "at least I hope you're likin' the food."

"It's actually not bad," Clint admitted.

"I assume you killed the rest of my men?" Quentin said to the sheriff.

"Actually," Clint said, "we let Skinner go after he told us where you were going."

"I shoulda killed him, myself," Quentin said. "You can't trust nobody these days."

"Ain't that the truth," Tatum said, pushing his empty plate away. "How many men you got waitin' outside for us?"

"Just two."

"And I can trust that you're tellin' the truth, right?" Tatum said.

"Of course," Quentin said. "They're gonna take care of you, and the Gunsmith, here, is mine."

"So when we walk out the door and the lead starts flying, they're going to be careful not to hit me," Clint said.

"They better be careful not to hit either one of us, Adams," Quentin said, good-naturedly.

"Then I guess we should all walk out together," Tatum suggested.

"That suits me," Quentin said. "I'm not lookin' to ambush you fellas. Fair's fair."

Clint and Tatum exchanged a glance. Clint wondered if this killer really wanted to face him man-to-man? Or were his men going to start shooting as soon as they walked out? And what about the men who worked for his friend, the town's owner?

"I assume breakfast was on you," Clint said.

"Of course," Quentin said. "I wanted to be the one to buy you your last meal."

"Who's this friend you talked about?" Tatum asked. "The one who owns the town?"

"His name's Aaron Pritchard."

Quentin could see that both Clint and Tatum recognized the name. It made him a bit jealous. But after today, everybody would know the name Max Quentin.

"But he's not involved in this," Quentin said. "He's just gonna watch, like everybody else." Quentin stood up. "Shall we go?"

Chapter Forty-Four

Clint was surprised when there were no shots fired as they exited the restaurant.

"This ain't a big town, as you can see," Quentin said, "but I still want to do this on the main street, so . . ."

"You wanna walk over there together?" Sheriff Tatum asked.

"I keep tellin' you this is gonna be fair," Quentin said.

"Three against two?" Tatum asked. "That's fair."

"Well," Quentin said, "I guess that's as fair as it's gonna get."

"And what about these houses that look down on the town?" Clint asked. "No rifles in the windows?"

"Not that I know of."

"And I suppose Pritchard's watching from one of them?" Clint asked.

"I'm sure he will be," Quentin said. "His is the biggest one up there."

Clint turned and looked up.

"Are we ready?" Quentin asked.

Was the man that confident, Clint wondered? He hoped so, because after all this time, he would like nothing better than to end this right in the street, no matter how many, or how few, witnesses there were.

***

From a second floor window of his house, Aaron Pritchard watched the main street. It occurred to him the action might not take place there, but he—as well as his men could pretty much see the entire little town from their vantage points.

His men had been ordered not to shoot unless he did. And his intention was to watch the action, not take part. But he knew when the action started, he might get the itch, so he had his rifle in his hands.

Just in case.

***

Clint and Tatum walked with Max Quentin until he turned down a very narrow side street. It was a perfect place for an ambush.

Quentin stopped and turned to face them.

"Comin'?" he asked.

"We'll go around the long way," Clint said.

"I don't like narrow streets like this," Tatum said.

"Well then," Quentin said, "see you on the other side."

He turned, went down the street that was little more than an alley, and out the other side. As Tatum started away, Clint stopped him.

"I suggest we go this way," he said.

"But we told him we were goin' around," the lawman pointed out.

"All the more reason we should go this way."

Tatum saw the wisdom in Clint's words, and agreed. They would not be expected to go this way.

When they came out the other end, they were on Churchill's main street. Max Quentin was standing with his two men, looking off down the street in the direction he thought they would be coming from.

"Quentin!" Clint called.

The three men turned and looked at Clint and Tatum, and the other two panicked. They reached for their guns, against Quentin's orders that he would draw first.

"No!" he shouted.

Clint and Tatum both drew and fired, once each, and both men fell to the ground on either side of their boss, leaving Quentin standing there alone.

***

Aaron Pritchard watched the two men fall and knew things hadn't gone as planned. And he also knew that he needed Quentin for the job in Denver.

He opened his window and stuck his rifle out. Across the way, his three men did the same.

***

Clint and Tatum holstered their weapons.

"You call this fair?" Quentin complained "Two against one?"

Tatum looked at Clint, who nodded. The lawman walked across the street, stepped up onto the boardwalk to watch.

"He'll stay out of it?" Quentin asked.

"He won't do a thing," Clint said.

"So that man I killed," Quentin said. "He wasn't your brother?"

"If he's who I think he was," Clint said, "No."

"Fine," Quentin said, "I'll stop sayin' I killed the Gunsmith's brother."

"Good."

"I'll just say I killed the Gunsmith."

But before either of them could draw their guns, the shots came from above.

Chapter Forty-Five

The sound came from rifles.

As Clint was afraid of, there were men in the houses with rifles. But while he had expected it, he saw that Quentin was surprised.

"What the hell—" Quentin said, ducking for cover.

Clint also scrambled for cover behind a buckboard as lead struck the ground all around him. He also saw Tatum drop down behind a horse trough.

The thing about Max Quentin, though, was that while he had ducked for cover, they were not shooting at him.

The shooting stopped, as they reloaded.

"So that's your friend?" Clint called out.

"He was supposed to stay out of it," Quentin called back. "I don't know what he's doin'."

"It's pretty obvious," Tatum yelled from his position. "They're tryin' to kill us."

"Not Quentin," Clint said. "None of the shots came near him."

"Is that right?" Quentin called out.

"Step out and see," Clint said.

After a few moments Quentin appeared, and stepped out into the street. There were no shots.

"See?" Clint said.

"He's just tryin' to help," Quentin said. "I'll wave him off."

He looked up at the biggest house and waved both hands.

"Okay," Quentin said, "you can step out."

Clint stuck his head out from behind the buckboard, and immediately there were half a dozen shots. He ducked back down.

"I don't think so, Quentin."

"Damn it!" Quentin yelled. "Aaron, what the hell—"

There were two more shots, but they didn't come near Quentin. Clint figured they were just supposed to draw him out.

"Aaron!" Quentin yelled. "He's mine!"

Then from above, a voice echoed.

"Get off the street, Max!" a man called. "We'll take care of this."

"Damn it!" Quentin said. He looked at Clint. "This isn't over!"

"You're leaving?" Clint asked.

"I just gotta get up to that house and tell Pritchard what he's up against."

As Quentin went running up the street Clint called out, "That's not going to make him stop!"

"We can't let him get away!" Tatum shouted. He started to break from cover, but rifle fire drove him back.

"I don't think he's trying to get away," Clint called out.

"Clint, you're closer to that alley we came down," Tatum shouted. "I'll cover you."

"At this range? With your pistol?"

"You got a better idea?"

"No," Clint admitted.

"The noise might just attract their attention. Then you can get closer to those houses and do some damage."

"Okay," Clint said. "on three. One . . . two . . . three!"

***

Max Quentin was both puzzled and annoyed. Pritchard had told him to take care of this himself, and that was what he had intended to do.

Now this?

He made his way up to Aaron Pritchard's house, aware of the shots still coming from the windows of *that* house, and the one on the other side. Sheriff Tatum and Adams were in a crossfire.

As Quentin made his way to Pritchard's house, he wondered what should be uppermost in his mind, killing the Gunsmith or the bank job in Denver. He had plenty of money from the Rock Springs job. He *could* be richer, but could he be bigger than the Man Who Killed The Gunsmith?

The answer to that was a resounding no.

***

Hannah Gill had come running into the room when she heard the shots. It had taken her a while to pinpoint it, but when she entered, she saw Pritchard hanging half out his window, with his rifle.

"What's going on?" she demanded.

Pritchard looked over his shoulder at her, raised his eyebrows and gave her a smile.

"Nothing that concerns you, sweetie," he said. "Why don't you go back to the bedroom and wait."

"I wasn't in the bedroom," she told him.

"Well. Go there!" he snapped. "I'm a little busy at the moment."

"Doing exactly what?" she asked. "Killing people from your window?"

"Not just people," he said, sighting along the barrel of his rifle. "Two people in particular."

Chapter Forty-Six

Clint felt sure that Quentin was going to the big house to confront his friend, Pritchard. So he decided to head for the other house. More shots were coming from there, where he figured there would be at last three shooters—the three men he and Tatum had seen in the saloon.

At the count of three he broke from cover as Tatum started shooting. Making it back down that small alley he started looking for a way to get up to that second house. He found a path he thought would do it and started to work his way up. Since Quentin already knew the way, he wondered if the man had made it to his goal?

He was very close to his own.

***

As Quentin reached Pritchard's house, he found the front door locked. Rather than look for another way in, he decided to kick it open. It worked on his third try, and he rushed in. Just at that moment, Hannah Gill was coming down the staircase.

"Where is he?" he yelled.

"Middle room, in front," she said. "He's gone crazy!"

Quentin ran up. As he entered the room, Pritchard was firing his rifle. Quentin ran up behind him, hauled him in from the window and grabbed the rifle from his hands.

"What the hell are you doin'?" he demanded. "You said you were gonna stay out of it."

"You need the help," Pritchard said, "and I need you for the Denver job. I can't have some sheriff putting a bullet in you."

"That's a sheriff," Quentin said, "and a Gunsmith."

"A what? A gunsmith?"

"Actually," Quentin said, "the Gunsmith."

Pritchard looked shocked.

"Clint Adams? He followed you here?"

"He did."

"Is this about that whole brother thing?"

"Yeah, it is."

"Jesus." Pritchard looked out the window as his men started firing from the house across the way. "We're going to need more men."

"No more men!" Quentin said. "I'll handle it myself."

"You're going to take the Gunsmith."

"Yeah, and you're gonna stay out of it."

"Are you kidding? That's the Gunsmith down there? I can have five more men here in an hour."

"No!" Quentin snapped. He pushed the rifle back into Pritchard's hand, then pushed again. The man went backward, hit the window sill, and fell out the window. It was a long way down to a small street in town.

***

Clint reached the house he wanted, saw the rifle barrels sticking out the window. He took a moment to fire up at the windows, knowing that he was closer. The barrels were withdrawn, as the men scrambled for cover.

In that moment Tatum would be able to break from cover and start up to join him, but he wasn't going to wait.

He found the front door, kicked it in and entered. As he did a man with a rifle was running down the stairs. They saw each other and both reacted, but Clint was faster. He fired, hitting the man dead center in the belly. He gasped, dropped the rifle, grabbed his belly, and fell down the rest of the stairs.

Clint paused to make sure he was dead, then ran up the stairs with the gun in his hands.

"Did you get him, Lonny?" someone yelled.

Clint found the room the voice had come out of.

"Sorry," he said, from the doorway, "Lonny can't answer."

These two were as stupid as most gunman. They both reacted immediately, starting to bring their rifles to bear on him. Clint wasted no time, shot them both. His bullet hit the first one in the belly, doubling him over and onto the floor. The other one was hit in the chest, driven back, and out the open window.

Clint went to the window to look down at the fallen man on the street below. At that moment he saw movement in a window cross the street, and then a man fell from that window, also all the way down to a town street below.

He assumed that was Pritchard.

He turned as he heard somebody in the hall. Sheriff Tatum came running in, gun in hand, looked down at the body on the floor.

"What happened?" he asked. "There's a dead body downstairs."

"And two outside," Clint said.

"What in the blazes—"

"I knew these big, old houses were dangerous," Clint said, reloading.

"Wha—"

Clint turned on Tatum, cutting him off.

"Let's go."

Chapter Forty-Seven

Assuming the body across the way was Pritchard, Clint and Tatum decided to return to the main street. On the way they stopped at the bodies of both men who had fallen from windows, to determine that they were, indeed, dead. When they reached the street, it was empty.

"If he's gone on the run again, we're gonna have to chase him through those mountains," Tatum complained.

"He won't run," Clint said. "He wants to end this as much as we do."

"I hope you're right."

Clint pointed up the street and said, "I think I am."

Tatum looked and saw Max Quentin walking toward them.

"You know," the lawman said, "we could kill him easy."

Clint shook his head.

"In a few years, hundreds of people are going to say they were here to see this," he said. "I can't tell you what to do when this is over, Sheriff, but for now you can step aside."

Tatum just nodded and stepped up onto the nearby boardwalk to watch.

Quentin kept coming until he was about ten feet away, then stopped.

"You pushed your friend out the window," Clint said.

"He wasn't my friend," Quentin said, "and besides, it was an accident—but he was butting into something that wasn't his business."

"You have a choice, Quentin," Clint said. "Go back to Rock Springs with the sheriff, or go for that gun."

"I think you know which one I favor," Quentin said, then looked at the lawman. "But I will tell the sheriff if you kill me, and he goes into Pritchard's house, he'll find the bank proceeds."

"That's decent of you," Tatum said.

"Yeah, but you gotta hope Adams kills me, because if I kill him, I'll kill you, next."

"I'll keep that in mind," Tatum said.

Quentin looked at Clint.

"Are you sure that fella I killed wasn't your brother?" he asked.

"Positive," Clint said. Even if the dead man had been a step-brother, Clint did not consider him—or anyone connected to the man who was cruel to his mother—to be family.

"Oh well . . ." Quentin said, and drew.

Clint had been watching very carefully for that hitch that most men had when they were about to draw their guns. The day he didn't see it was the day he might've been outdrawn, but that wasn't today.

As Quentin fell backward onto the ground, dead before he landed, Tatum stepped off the boardwalk and said to Clint, "Let's go up to that house and get that money."

Coming February 27, 2020

THE GUNSMITH
456
The Daughter of Jean Lafitte

For more information
click here: www.SpeakingVolumes.us

Coming Soon!

Lady Gunsmith
9
Roxy Doyle and the Lady Executioner

For more information
visit: www.SpeakingVolumes.us

On Sale Now!

Lady Gunsmith
8
Roxy Doyle and the Silver Queen

**For more information
click here:** www.SpeakingVolumes.us

On Sale Now!

Lady Gunsmith *series*
Books 1-7

www.ingramcontent.com/pod-product-compliance
Lightning Source LLC
Chambersburg PA
CBHW020558250626
47154CB00004B/1271